23 SHADOW STREET
CASE FILES

BOOK ONE
DEADLY DREAMS

By
BARBARA STEINER

ibooks
DISTRIBUTED BY PUBLISHERS GROUP WEST

A Publication of ibooks, inc.

Distributed by:
Publishers Group West
1700 Fourth Street, Berkeley, CA 94710

ibooks, inc.
24 West 25th Street
New York, NY 10010

ISBN 1-59687-329-9
First ibooks, inc. printing March 2006
10 9 8 7 6 5 4 3 2 1

Printed in the U.S.A.

DEDICATION

FOR SUSAN LYNDS, good friend and biggest fan.

"… wicked dreams abuse the curtained sleep…"
Macbeth
William Shakespeare

Chapter 1

Don't look now," Sadi Sun, Alexa's best friend, whispered, keeping hold of Alexa's arm and steering her toward her locker. "But Peter Talbott is heading right this way, and I don't think he wants to talk to me."

Alexa's heart raced, despite her telling herself she didn't care if Peter existed. She did care. She had been secretly watching him for a long time, going to the jazz band concerts where he played piano, staring at the back of his head in the classes they had together. But she didn't think he knew *she* existed.

"I can't believe it," Peter said, his deep voice surrounding Alexa like a net. She couldn't have run if she'd wanted to. "Have I finally got you cornered?" His smile was easy, confident, and totally sexy.

Alexa turned around, trying to act casual, wishing she'd paid more attention to the way she'd dressed today, although she did have on low-rider jeans and a favorite rust-colored cropped top. Her ponytail brushed her long, dark hair across her shoulders as she turned. She also wished she wasn't so tall that she stood almost eye-to-eye with Peter.

She was sure Peter dated anytime he pleased, but he didn't hang with any girl in the halls like the other rich, popular guys did. Peter was well known as a loner. He was quiet, smart, and drop-dead, Tom-Cruise gorgeous. Usually his rich, coffee-colored eyes reflected one message. *Don't even think of speaking to me.*

Right now they said, *I'm dying to get to know you better.* Alexa felt her face heating up, but kept her own gaze neutral, trying to decide what to do about his attention. What could he possibly want with her? Why would he want to get to know her better?

Not that Alexa was a nerd or goth or weird. But only Sadi kept her from being a loner herself. Her mother had been sick for so long, she hadn't had time to date. And often her father needed computer help with some of his cases. Then, after her mother died, she'd concentrated on her classes and being there for her dad and her younger sister, Emma.

"Hi, Peter. What's up?" Alexa stepped back a little, right into Sadi, who pinched her.

"What's up is a party. Not mine, not for me. Wait. I'm not saying this right." Peter closed his eyes and ran his hand through his hair. "I'm not used to being in the company of two beautiful women."

He could lie smoothly. She'd give him that.

Sadi pinched her again. Alexa didn't dare look at Sadi, knowing she'd totally lose her composure and giggle. *Please, God, don't let me giggle.*

"I'll start over." He took a deep breath and smiled again. "Would you like to come to a party at my house Saturday night? It's a party for my sister, Lexie's, sixteenth birthday, and my mother asked me to be there. I'd love it if you'd say yes."

"As protection or to help you chaperone or—"

"Right on, Alexa. I'm actually panic-stricken to be there alone."

They all laughed, and Alexa relaxed a little. She spoke before she could think about this unexpected event. "The experience could be enlightening. And my sister, Emma, is going, I'm sure. Lexie's her best friend."

Peter's brilliant smile would have made her agree to almost anything. "Okay, I'll pick you up at seven tomorrow night. You, too, Sadi. Both of you come, and yes, Emma, of course. Lexie can't survive," Peter stretched out the end of the word, "without her three best friends, Emma, Amber, and Brianna. Why is it that fifteen-year-old girls run in packs?"

"The better to search out prey and eat them alive." Alexa laughed at Peter, who hardly said anything and who was now babbling. Peter Talbott babbling? Hell really was going to freeze over, but she hoped that wouldn't happen until after Lexie's party.

Peter dragged his hand through curly, dark brown hair and waved as he left them standing in the hall, staring at his back. A very nice back it was. The thin, faded, Blues Brother t-shirt he wore only served to emphasize his muscles. How do you get that kind of muscles playing a piano?

"I don't know if I want to go out with Peter Talbott, Sadi." Alexa leaned on her locker and watched Peter hurry away from her. "I wish I hadn't said yes. I've fantasized about his noticing me for so long, now that he has, I'm scared."

"The confident and capable Alexa Kane is scared? You're just inexperienced. Or more like socially inept. Dating impaired. You've got to start going on real dates soon. And what's not to like about Peter Talbott? Are you going to spend the rest of the year sneaking into his jazz concerts and staring at his back?"

Sadi sighed and shook her head. Then she smoothed down her short, black, pixie-cut hair. Her nearly black eyes sparkled. "Half the girls at Stuyvesant would die for a chance to date Peter."

"Maybe that's my problem. Daydreaming about him is one thing. But do I want to go out with a guy that popular, a guy who draws girls like the Pied Piper draws rats?"

Sadi laughed. "Peter plays piano, Al, not a flute."

"Oh, why am I worried? It's not really a date." Alexa swung her heavy backpack onto her shoulder, deploring the fact that this was Friday. She shouldn't have to study on a weekend. "You heard him. He just asked me if I'd like to come to Lexie's birthday party and help him keep an eye on a house full of fifteen- and sixteen-year-old kids."

"Then added me as an afterthought. That's not *my* idea of a date." Sadi dropped her pack, jumped into a karate stance, chopped the air, then grabbed the bookbag up again. "And I hope you don't expect me to go with you. I'm getting my black belt tomorrow, remember?"

"Of course, I remember. You'd have gotten yours when I did if you hadn't been sick with mono. "Are you ready?" That was a silly question. When was Sadi not ready for any test?

They continued talking as they left the school and walked past the art galleries of SoHo. SoHo was an acronym for "south of Houston," a street in Lower Manhattan. It was one of the hippest neighborhoods in New York City, a mecca of trendy shops, chic restaurants, and avant garde art shows.

Alexa peeked into the Cyber Café, but the place was way too crowded to go in. They paused to look in the windows of a store called Evolution, where masks for Halloween were already featured in the windows. A skeleton seemed to grin at Alexa, mocking her worries about Peter.

"We could consult 'The SoHo Psychic,'" Sadi suggested. They passed by the psychic's store every day. Both girls had promised themselves a visit, but neither had gotten up the funds or the nerve.

Sadi didn't believe in the psychic world anyway. She was very well grounded. Mercedes "Sadi" Sun was proficient in Chinese, a computer genius, made straight As, aced the SATs, and had a dozen colleges courting her. She and Alexa had been best friends since first grade. Standing next to each other, they looked like a bad case of opposites attract, but they had been the same size when they were six. Now Alexa was five-nine and Sadi was five-four. That should have given Alexa an advantage, but when they were sparring together, Sadi usually won. She was quicker and more agile. Unless she really concentrated, Alexa was clumsy. She hoped it was a stage she was going through because she had grown tall so fast.

"I've been ready to get this belt for a long time. You know that, Al."

"On Saturday morning, my karate students are testing for their yellow belts at eight, and I have to be there for them. But I'll be finished in plenty of time to come with you to your test. Then, you're going with me to the party." Alexa made her voice sound like a command, when it was really a plea for help. She, who thought she wasn't afraid of anything, was nervous over a sort-of date with Peter Talbott. "We can sneak out early and get a cab home if we get bored."

Sadi shrugged, as if she knew she couldn't say no to Alexa. Sadi was pretty easy going compared to how intense Alexa was, without always meaning to be. Her mother used to point this out to Alexa often enough. Relax, Al, relax. The mantra had become ingrained in Alexa's mind, for what good it was worth.

They stopped at Alexa's building. Alexa was eager to get out of the traffic, which seemed louder than usual, more annoying. Although she loved living in the city, she had a low tolerance for noise.

Alexa's loft apartment, a short distance from school, was in an old cast-iron warehouse. She liked to think about the artists who converted the building into lofts in the 1960s, often living there with no heat. Alexa's father, Tony, and her mother, Sylvia, had found the place when the neighborhood was marginal and the apartment trashed out. Otherwise, they never could have afforded it. The loft was worth a fortune now, but her dad said he wouldn't think of selling it. He liked living in the city, and he liked for the girls to be able to walk to school.

Alexa liked her address: 23 Shadow Street. And New York City had an energy all its own, day and night. She fed on that energy and made it hers.

She and Sadi stepped into the huge elevator that made the loft accessible to her father in his wheelchair and felt it rumble under their feet as it wobbled to the third floor. Alexa had her key ready and let them in. The Kane apartment opened onto one big room, divided by partitions or arrangements of furniture.

"Dad's not home." Alexa tossed her jean jacket on a chair by the door. She could always tell. There were no spicy smells of meatballs in tomato sauce, spaghetti, or lasagna. No jazz hummed through the sparsely furnished, bare-floored space, designed to accommodate his wheelchair. The apartment had a hollow, empty feel.

She and Sadi grabbed a bag of chips and drinks and hurried to Alexa's room, a real room with a door. As Alexa and Emma got older, they had insisted on some privacy. Their mother had agreed. One of her dad's buddies, who was good at carpentry, created a space for both girls, as well as a closed bedroom for her mother and father.

"You'd think you were allergic to sunlight," Sadi complained, running up the shades on two windows, making Alexa squint, despite the growing shadows of late afternoon.

Alexa did like her room cool and dark and quiet. It was a place to hide, a place to recover when the world was too much with her, as some poet, she could never remember who, had said. She had decorated it in forest green, navy, and burgundy. She dropped her books in a corner, stretched out on her futon bed, which was piled with fuzzy pillows, and sighed. Immediately her cat, Black Bart, found her. Bart butted his head against Alexa's chin, rubbed back and forth against her arm, and purred so loud that Sadi laughed.

"I'd say Bart is glad to see you."

"Always." Alexa hugged Bart to her stomach, loving his silky fur. She listened to the click of her computer keys as Sadi checked out a site she said she was curious about. And she tried to imagine what a real date with Peter Talbott would be like.

They got through Saturday with Sadi the proud possessor of a black belt in Tae Kwon Do. Now they could both start on their degrees. Alexa's class of beginners all did her proud and all got their yellow belts. Alexa felt energized and confident after the demo of sparring she and Sadi put on for the parents. She hoped a party would be a fun way to top off a perfect day.

Back at the loft, Emma strolled into the kitchen to get a bottle of water.

"When did you get your bellybutton pierced?" Alexa asked.

She wanted to bite her tongue. Here she was being mother to Emma again. Emma was dressed in a tiny skirt about nine inches from waist to hem. The pink tank with spaghetti straps didn't meet the skirt waist, leaving a four-inch band of flesh exposed at Emma's middle. And without asking, Emma had sneaked out and gotten her bellybutton pierced.

"We all did it together." Emma stood in the kitchen, one hip cocked to the right while she sipped the bottled spring water. "Whatta you care?"

Alexa took a deep breath. What if Emma had asked her opinion about body piercing? Alexa knew most of the girls her age did it. Did she have a right to tell Emma not to? "I was just surprised. Did it hurt? Where's Dad?"

"Yes, it hurt. And Dad called. Said he was tied up with work for another couple of hours. Why are you dressed up?" Emma's frown was suspicious.

"Would it surprise you to know I have a date?" If Alexa had to chose one word to describe her relationship with her sister, she'd say abrasive. Emma had a knack for rubbing her the wrong way with everything she said. "Peter Talbott. He's picking us all up in half hour."

"Us? You're going to *my* party?" Emma set the bottle down so hard that water jetted out the top.

"Why not?"

"I don't need a chaperone."

"Peter invited me. So it's my party, too."

Emma glared at Alexa. "Whatever." She shook her long blonde hair, which tonight she had twisted into a hundred or so curls, whirled, and hurried back to her room.

When had Emma gotten so cute, so sexy? Alexa had to admit Emma was totally teen-model material. While she didn't want to take on the role of guarding Emma, maybe it was good she was going to this party to keep an eye on her. She wished her father was here to tell Emma she looked way too sexy for fifteen. But he wasn't, and if he was, would he even notice? And would he say anything?

Three years ago, after their mother died, Alexa's father had left the parenting of Emma up to Alexa. She knew he was still grieving himself, but parenting Emma was an impossible task. Emma resented everything Alexa said to her, usually saying she was old enough to take care of herself.

What could Alexa do? Not much. Look after herself. She had dressed in her favorite jeans, a lime-green top with spaghetti straps only a couple shades lighter than her eyes, and big gold hoops in her ears. She let her long, brown hair hang loose. Sometimes when the light caught it right, the red highlights kept it from being mousy. She decided on black flats, clipping a shiny lime-green buckle onto the front of each. They weren't as sexy as Emma's medium-heel sandals, but if Alexa wore heels, she'd tower over Peter. And there was the clumsy factor to keep in mind. Unless she stumbled and accidently fell into Peter's arms. No, too embarrassing.

Looking in the mirror, she grabbed her new houndstooth newsboy cap, her one concession to style this year. She liked the way it made her look sexy if she cocked her head. Would Peter think she was sexy? OMIGOD, did she care? If she did, she was already in trouble. She had never been one to obsess over her looks. Or stand at the mirror for hours like Emma did. She wasn't going to start now.

The sky was clear for a change, and stars winked at them as they popped from black velvet like sequins. The evening was warm, a perfect curtain coming down on a perfect fall day. Peter and Sadi arrived at the same time.

"I called a cab, since Mother is already freaking out."

He looked at Alexa, and she shivered. Again she thought the evening might be more fun than she had anticipated. She was glad she'd said yes to Peter, even under the circumstances. This would give her a chance to get to know him, to feel comfortable with him. Then maybe he'd invite her on a real date. Nothing at school, she hoped, but the theater or a nice restaurant.

When the taxi pulled up, Peter put Emma, Sadi and Alexa in the back, and he got in the front with the driver. No one said anything once Peter gave the address, and Alexa was glad the trip wasn't long. When the car stopped, Emma jumped out and ran on inside. She probably didn't want anyone to know she'd come with her sister.

The party was raving when Peter opened the door and they entered a rather ordinary two-story brownstone in the West Village. Inside, the house was beautifully decorated with gleaming hardwood floors. Furniture was sparse and contemporary, mostly black leather. Large windows would give the rooms a open and airy feel by day. On one wall hung a large abstract painting of black, white, red, and magenta. Alexa suspected the Talbotts had bought the house, which might have been several apartments, put it back together as one residence, and spared no expense on furniture, art, and some rather strange sculptures.

As with most old houses, though, there were lots of nooks and crannies. Most of them were already full of couples making out or foursomes laughing and passing drinks and smokes around. Some of the smoke had a sweet smell that Alexa recognized, but it wasn't her place to say anything.

"Mother said she was going to trust everyone," Peter whispered in her ear. "I think she's a little naive."

"Where's your dad?"

"Where else? Out of town on business." Peter laughed but not with humor. "Let's find something to drink. I only said I'd be here, so we can hang wherever we like. Shoot pool?"

As a matter of fact, Alexa did. Her father had been teaching her when she was eleven, just before his accident. He said she was a natural. Truth was, she worshiped her father. She would have tried any game or sport he suggested, just to spend time with him. He had kept taking her to the pool hall where off-duty police hung out, even when he could no longer play. And lots of his buddies on the force were willing to coach Alexa.

Peter let her break, and when she sunk half the balls before she missed, he whistled. "I guess you do. What other hidden talents do you have?"

Alexa smiled as Sadi missed after sinking two and Peter got a turn. "I'm into karate, Tae Kwon Do, to be exact."

"Yeah, I heard about that. First-degree black belt. Quiet and lethal. Is that why you aren't dating anyone?"

"Who says I'm not dating?" Alexa looked at Sadi, who was cracking up behind a can of Coke.

"I asked around. I never invite a girl to help me chaperone birthday parties unless I check her out." Peter grinned and Alexa felt drawn in despite planning to be careful around him.

Peter sighted in on the eight ball, sunk it, then ran the rest of the table. He was racking another set of balls when Emma found them.

"Al, I need help. Lexie needs help." Emma looked at Peter, but she grabbed hold of Alexa's arm. "Come quick. I think she's in trouble."

"Where is she?" Peter asked.

"In her bathroom." Emma led the way upstairs, pulling Alexa along with her.

Lexie was sitting on the bathroom floor, surrounded by empty plastic water bottles. "I'm so cold, so cold." Lexie's blonde hair hung across her face in wet tangles. "First I was hot, now I'm freezing. Help me, Peter, help me."

"What did you take?" Peter squatted beside her. "Did you take any drugs?"

Lexie shook her head and grabbed an empty bottle. "I'm thirsty. Get me some more water, Emma."

"You've already had a lot of water, Lexie. Maybe too much." Emma huddled by the sink, her hands in fists against her mouth.

"What did Lexie take?" Alexa grabbed both of Emma's arms. She wanted to shake her, but knew that would do no good. "Did you take anything, Emma? What did Lexie take?"

Emma started to cry. Alexa pushed her into Lexie's bedroom. Brianna Sasa and Amber Quint, part of the fearsome foursome, as Alexa sometimes called them, sat on Lexie's bed sniffling. Alexa stared at them. They were obviously terrified.

"What did Lexie take?" Alexa raised her voice just below a shout. This time she did shake Emma. Emma broke into full-out sobbing, but she held out her hand. A little damp, a little smudged, but the cloverleaf-shaped drug, missing one leaf, was easily recognizable.

Ecstasy.

Chapter 2

"Get my mother," Peter said, stepping into the bedroom and grabbing a comforter off the bed. "I'm calling an ambulance." He grabbed Lexie's cell phone, which was lying on her bedside table.

Emma ran back to stay with Lexie. Alexa and Sadi started the search for Mrs. Talbott. God, the house was big, much bigger than it looked from outside. Alexa ran up and down the stairs, looking into every room. Finally, in the back of the house, she found a beautiful kitchen with cherry wood cabinets and black granite counters.

A woman, holding a martini glass and perched on a bar stool, was laughing and talking to someone on the phone. Tall and thin, she wore tight black slacks that slimmed down to fit the ankle, and a cotton knit top covered with a pattern of black and gray bugle beads. Long black chandelier earrings dangled almost to her shoulders. She had kicked off one three-inch high heel sandal and hooked the other on a rung of the stool. Her hair, twisted into a knot on top of her head, was kept blonde by an expensive beauty salon. Lexie would look exactly like her in twenty years.

Mrs. Talbott set down her glass and filled it again from a pitcher on the counter, still not seeing Alexa or being aware she wasn't alone. Alexa suspected Mrs. Talbott had resorted to the liquor in order to survive chaperoning the birthday party.

Alexa touched her arm to get her attention. "Mrs. Talbott, we need you. Lexie's sick."

"What do you mean, Lexie's sick? Where is she?" Mrs. Talbott took a big slug of the liquor and set the martini glass on the counter. "I'll call you back." She set the phone in its cradle, slipped into her second shoe, and followed Alexa as Alexa told her what she knew.

"Lexie has probably taken some drugs, Mrs. Talbott. Maybe an overdose. Peter's with her, but she needs you."

"Taken some drugs? That's not true. Lexie doesn't take drugs. You must be mistaken."

Alexa wished she was. She kept quiet and stepped aside so Lexie's mother could go into Lexie's bathroom. Peter was again sitting beside Lexie on the floor. He had wrapped her in the comforter.

"Hang on, Lex. Just hang on. We're getting you help."

Mrs. Talbott screamed and crouched by Lexie. "Lexie, please, what's wrong? Did you take something? What did you take?" When Lexie didn't respond, Mrs. Talbott shook her gently, then harder.

Mrs. Talbott was a psychologist, so surely she'd had some medical training, but sometimes when the patient is close to you, you can't see the problem.

"Carry her down to the front door, Peter," Alexa said, kneeling beside Lexie and trying to take her pulse. "We need to hurry. I think she's passed out."

"Wait, who are you?" Mrs. Talbott grabbed Alexa's arm. She looked frightened and angry at the same time. "Did you give Lexie drugs? Is that how you know she took something?"

Stay calm, Alexa advised herself and took a deep breath. "I'm Alexa Kane, Mrs. Talbott, Emma's sister. I'm here as a guest of Peter's. We don't know where Lexie got the drug, just that she took it. Don't you want to go in the ambulance to the hospital? I'll stay here, ask everyone to leave, and lock up the house. You need a coat, your purse."

Mrs. Talbott got up and ran back downstairs as if she heard none of what Alexa had said. Peter carried Lexie down behind her. Alexa crumpled into a heap, feeling helpless. Sadi squeezed Alexa's arm. In minutes Peter was back. Alexa got to her feet.

"Mom went with Lexie. Help me get all these kids out of here, Alexa, Sadi. I'll call a taxi to take you home and then go to the hospital."

"I'm going with you to the hospital," Emma said. She had been so quiet, Alexa had forgotten she was there.

"Emma, where did Lexie get Ecstasy?" Alexa said, grabbing her arm. "Did you take any?"

Emma shook loose, turned away, and ran to talk to Brianna and Amber, who kept shaking their heads and crying.

Even with the three of them working, it took forever to ask all the party guests to leave. Some were half drunk or wobbly with something, others were laughing and giggling and protesting leaving a good party.

"If there's anyone else here passed out in a closet, I'm locking them in." Peter was ready to leave. Alexa and Sadi followed him outside to the cab he'd called and jumped in.

"I'm riding with Brianna and Amber," Emma called to them and got into the cab her friends had waiting.

"Doesn't your family have a car?" Sadi asked, as the cab pulled out to race through late evening traffic.

"Yes, but my dad only drives it when he has to leave the city. I think he's in New Jersey. Mom can call him from the hospital if she feels she needs him to come home."

There was a slight hint of bitterness in Peter's voice. Alexa interpreted it to mean that he thought his dad should have come home for Lexie's sixteenth birthday.

"Where do you think Lexie got drugs?" Alexa asked. Peter sat beside her, and she was aware of how tense he was.

"I don't know," Peter said. "Someone may have been dealing tonight. Ecstasy is easy to get. And dealing brings in big bucks until someone gets caught. Quite often, even then, he only gets a slap on the hand."

Alexa knew that some of the high school kids were probably dealing, but she had always ignored it. She didn't figure she could do anything about it, and she never thought it would make any difference in her life. She could barely entertain the idea that Emma was taking drugs. But if Lexie was, what would stop Emma?

At the hospital, the emergency room was busy on a Saturday night. They jumped out, Peter handed the driver a bill and took off, Alexa and Sadi right behind him.

He inquired at the desk, and they soon found Mrs. Talbott. She was sitting on an uncomfortable-looking orange couch, her head in her hands, crying.

"Mother, what is it? What did they say?" Peter sat beside her and put his arm around her.

"Oh, Peter, Lexie is in a coma. The doctor said we'd just have to wait and see what happens next. He wants to talk to you and Lexie's friends."

By the time the doctor had talked to Peter, Emma, Amber, and Brianna had come into the waiting room. "You need to talk to the doctor, Emma," Alexa said, taking a gentle hold on Emma's arm. The cute, sexy girl was gone. Emma's face was streaked with tears and mascara, her eyes red from crying.

"What can I tell him?" Emma said, her voice soft and shaky.

"Anything you know." Alexa pushed her toward where Peter and the doctor were standing.

"You were at the party?" The doctor was young, but forceful. His flinty blue eyes bored right into Emma. He was clearly angry but trying to contain his emotions. "She took Ecstasy?"

"Yes, we thought it was safe. She wanted it for her birthday. To celebrate turning sixteen. She said she heard that taking Ecstasy gave a person dreams, sweet dreams. She had been having a lot of bad dreams lately."

"No drug is safe, and Ecstasy is exceptionally unpredictable. The tablet could have been mixed with something else. She drank a lot of water? How much?"

"A lot. Maybe gallons." Emma's voice wobbled. "That's all she wanted. She kept saying she was hot and thirsty and the water made her feel better."

Emma collapsed in Alexa's arms while Amber and Brianna talked to the doctor. Alexa held on tight until Emma stopped shaking. "Emma, you said Lexie wanted Ecstacy for her birthday. Where did she get it? Do you know who she bought it from?"

"She—she didn't buy it. We did."

"You did? What do you mean?"

"Amber, Brianna, and I bought it for her. We got it from a girl at school. That's all Lexie said she wanted for a present. We didn't know… we thought it was safe. I took part of a tablet myself, but Lexie took half, then when nothing happened, she swallowed the rest of it a little while later."

"You took some yourself?" Alexa wanted to cry, too. She wanted someone to hold her and tell her she wasn't partly responsible for what was happening. Why hadn't she paid closer attention to what Emma was doing?

"Yes, just a tiny bite. I was scared to take more."

"Emma, get hold of yourself. We're going to have to go talk to the police. You need to tell them who you got the drug from. And you're going to have to admit that you and Amber and Brianna are partly responsible for what's happening to Lexie."

Six days later, Mr. and Mrs. Talbott, after practically living at the hospital, took Lexie off life support. She had never come out of the coma she had slipped into at the party. The coroner ruled her death was caused by water intoxication, her thirst triggered by taking the drug Ecstasy.

Emma was inconsolable. She locked herself in her room, and if she came out at all, it was at night or while Alexa or her father was gone.

Alexa tried to talk to her through the door. Emma either yelled, "Go away!" or said nothing. Often Alexa heard her crying.

"Emma, you're making yourself sick. Come out and talk or eat something. Let us help you."

"Leave her alone, Al," her father finally said. "Let her cry it out. She won't stay in there forever."

I would, Alexa thought. If I'd been a part of killing my best friend, of killing Sadi… Alexa couldn't even imagine how she'd feel, what she'd do.

Locked in her own room, Alexa let herself get into the quicksand of *What If?*

What if she'd have asked Emma what she'd gotten Lexie for her birthday? It was a purely hypothetical question, of course. Emma would never have said, "We got her some drugs. All she wanted was drugs, Ecstasy."

It's easy to think of something you might have said or done to prevent a useless death. After the fact. It's also useless brain wandering. Lexie wanted water. Alexa would have given her water. Who knew you could die from drinking too much water?

What if? What if?

What if Alexa had stayed with Emma instead of going off to shoot pool with Peter? That was an even sillier idea, since no way would the fearless four have let Alexa hang out with them.

Nor would I have wanted to do so. I wanted to be with Peter. Will I want to be with him again? Can I handle being with him now?

There were no answers to any of the questions Alexa asked herself. There were never any answers to useless questions.

Chapter 3

The service for Lexie Talbott was the second worst experience of Alexa's life. The first, of course, was her mother's funeral, but in some ways they'd had time to prepare for that. How do you prepare yourself for your mother dying? The idea took shape and became real as, over time, her mother got thinner, more frail, almost lost in her bed. Then, when she was hooked up to tubes and a machine was helping her breathe, the next step was a blessing. There had been time to say goodbye to her mother, time to accept the reality.

There was no time to accept Lexie's death. The Talbotts hadn't been able to say good-bye to Lexie. They hadn't expected to lose their daughter this way.

Emma sat between Sadi and Alexa. At first she clutched her hands together in her lap. Then she took hold of Alexa's hand and squeezed it tight. Alexa squeezed back, knowing that while Emma was thinking of Lexie, in her heart the death of their mother was still raw and painful. Sadi leaned over and put her arm around Emma.

Alexa had told Sadi that she didn't have to go to the funeral with them. But Sadi said anything that happened to Alexa's family happened to her, too. She wanted to be there to support Emma.

Emma had been only three years old when Alexa and Sadi became best friends. Often the two of them took care of Emma so Mrs. Kane could get some work done. Alexa's mother had said that curiosity was a sign of intelligence, so Emma must be off the IQ charts. She emptied the kitchen cupboards, banged on pots with spoons, and when Mrs. Kane took her out of the kitchen, Emma went into the closets and dresser drawers. Alexa and Sadi laughed as they tried to keep up with Emma, but the truth was that they sometimes helped her when she got to the closets. Dressing up in Mrs. Kane's clothes was their favorite thing to do.

Alexa dabbed at her eyes with a wadded-up handkerchief, remembering.

Sadi's parents were very strict, old-school Chinese. But Sadi didn't continue coming to Alexa's house to get away from discipline. She had plenty of her own, was as hard on herself as her parents.

Sadi hung out with the Kanes because she loved them like family. She felt comfortable with them. Alexa's mother and father both made her a part of all their activities. Sadi had made the right decision to be here today.

The closed casket at the front of the church was too large, too obvious, too cold. A photo of Lexie, a glamour photo where Lexie looked much older than fifteen, stared out at them, one dimensional and fake with a frozen smile and no life.

Alexa closed her eyes, took deep breaths, listened to the minister's words without hearing. The family skipped the part where friends and family spoke about memories of the deceased. No one felt they could talk without breaking down.

Few people in New York City have a car. They took the subway or a bus or a taxi to work. Mr. Kane could have gotten a van rigged so he could drive, but he hadn't driven anything but a cop car before his accident, so he felt no need to have transportation now. They had taken a cab to the church for the funeral, but Mr. Kane had called one of his friends to take them to the cemetery.

The day was golden. Crisp clean air surrounded them. Birds sang in the big trees, unaware that silence was called for. The grave side ceremony was short, so most people attending stood behind the chairs set out for family.

An itchy feeling made Alexa shiver. She looked around. Everyone stood, eyes to the ground or looking ahead to the family and the dark hole where the casket would be lowered after they left. The scent of too many flowers, sprays of roses, baskets of carnations and white orchids surrounded them, cloying, unnatural.

Carefully, Alexa glanced around again. Not everyone had come here from the church after the service. The gathering was small. There were kids from school with their families, all looking awkward and unnatural in formal clothing. A few police, not in uniform, but easily singled out by someone like Alexa who knew the persona, hovered at the perimeter of the actual grieving friends and family.

Why were the police here? Because Lexie died of a drug overdose? But why would that make this a police matter? Whoever supplied the drugs would certainly not come to the funeral. Would they?

The presence, the idea that someone was watching her, wouldn't go away. Why would anyone be out here, looking at Alexa? This wasn't about her. It wasn't even about Emma. It was about kids making a tragic mistake. A life cut short by well-meaning friends.

Alexa didn't think she had a speck of psychic power. She'd never had a dream that came true, never any insight or warning about a future event. She wasn't even sure she believed in such things. Why wouldn't this shivery feeling go away?

She continued to glance around furtively, not wanting to show any disrespect to the Talbott family. Still she saw no one looking at her. She saw hardly anyone she knew or had seen before.

She was relieved when the minister said "amen" to words she hadn't heard. The small crowd relaxed, whispered, drifted away. Emma hugged Brianna and Amber, then ran back and stood beside Alexa and Sadi again. She waited for someone to tell her what to do next.

Alexa, Mr. Kane, Sadi, and Emma went back to the loft apartment after the funeral service. Emma rushed straight into her room and closed her door. She had kept herself locked up almost full time since the party.

Alexa looked at her father, whose brown eyes were sad. Alexa knew the service had triggered for him thoughts of burying his wife. Half of Alexa's tears at the funeral were for her mother, a wound reopened by another death of someone so young.

"What can we do for Emma?" Sadi asked, and Alexa felt good that Sadi had said *we*. That also said she was a part of the Kane family and had been for a long time.

"Nothing," Tony Kane said. "Let her grieve. I think there was a grief counselor at school, but Emma wasn't there. I'll find out if she can talk to Emma alone."

"What's going to happen to Emma, Amber, and Brianna, Mr. Kane?" Sadi asked. "They gave Lexie the drug."

"I'm not sure, since they're underage, and they weren't exactly dealing." Tony Kane pressed his fist against his lips, and Alexa knew her father was trying not to break down crying. "Something, some sentence. Maybe probation and community service. This may sound strange, but being punished will help Emma. She wants to be punished."

Alexa understood what her father was saying. When she was little, and went to the Catholic church with her mother, she'd think up a list of bad things she had done when she went to confession so she could be forgiven. She always felt better afterwards. Now she knew life wasn't that simple.

Emma would never really forgive herself for helping cause Lexie's death, but talking about it to a stranger would help. Alexa hadn't been able to get Emma to talk to her or even unlock her door all week.

"Come and help me cook dinner, Alexa," Mr. Kane invited. "You, too, Sadi. You're way too thin."

Sadi laughed. Mr. Kane said that at least once a week, and he made sure Sadi ate with them often. They all headed for the kitchen corner of the big room.

Mr. Kane had always done half the cooking in their family. His parents and grandparents were Italian, and mealtime was an important part of the day. After his accident, he'd had some of the kitchen counters built lower to accommodate his wheelchair. Pots and pans hanging over the stove were on a rope-and-pulley system so he could lower whatever he needed.

A thunderstorm rumbled outside, turning the sky dark early in the afternoon. Dad pulled out candles and lit them all around the kitchen and in the dining area. He dimmed all the lights. Always a fan of the right atmosphere, he looked over his collection of jazz and put on a Miles Davis' *Kind of Blue*. The room filled with the soft, mellow sounds of trumpet.

Tears came to Alexa's eyes as she and Sadi rolled meatballs from the mixture Mr. Kane had pulled from the fridge and set before them at the big round table. The kitchen began to smell of tomato sauce, sweet basil, rosemary, and thyme. Dad stuck the aniseed under their noses before he dumped a couple of teaspoons into the pot.

"Are we expecting company?" Alexa asked, eyeing the huge quantity of sauce.

Dad shrugged. "Leftovers all week. Sauce gets better with age." He stirred the meatballs in a skillet as Alexa and Sadi finished rolling them out. The meat browned, sizzled, and smelled delicious.

Sadi got out plates, looked at Alexa, who nodded, and set the table for four. Emma was still locked in her room, but maybe the smells would slip under her door and tempt her. Spaghetti in the pot of boiling water, French bread, buttered and sprinkled with garlic salt in the lower oven, everything was coming to a perfect finish. Alexa hadn't felt she could eat today when the funeral service finished. They stopped at Lexie's house for a very short time, then had been relieved to come home.

Dad and the thunderstorm, which had settled to steady rain, changed their mood. Alexa was serving plates when she heard a familiar sound. Emma's door creaked. Not saying anything, Alexa filled the fourth plate and set it back on the table.

Emma slipped into her seat and took her red checkered napkin. Her hair was piled on top of her head in a soft, ragged blonde mop. She wore no makeup, and looked as if she were about ten years old. "What's going to happen to me, Daddy? What's going to happen next?"

Mr. Kane took a bite of meatball, swirled spaghetti around his fork, tasted it, nodded at the food, pronounced it perfect. "I don't know, Sweetie. But we're with you on this. You made a mistake. You paid too big a price already. We'll stand behind you whatever happens next."

Alexa paused before she took another bite of dinner. She was flooded with emotion. Anger for anyone who thought dealing drugs to high school kids was a valid way to make a buck, a terrible sadness that her mother was missing from this table, love for her father and her best friend, Sadi, and an overwhelming empathy for Emma, who would be asking for forgiveness her entire life.

Two days later, in a pouring rain, Alexa and Sadi headed for Alexa's place, as was their habit, since there's was something good to eat. They burst into the living room, laughing, shaking off water, throwing jackets and books onto the closest chair.

"Oh-oh," Sadi said, grabbing her things back up, pulling the door back open. "See you later, Al."

Alexa didn't even say good-bye. She was frozen, staring at her dad and two suits, obviously waiting for her to come home. Both men wore their business smiles along with their "I'm important" airs.

"Alexa, come on in here. These men have an idea that I think is very sound. And we all want to talk to you."

Chapter 4

The men with Alexa's dad weren't any she'd ever seen before. They were not his pals who still came around, ordered pizza, played poker, listened to jazz. That was probably why Sadi had left so abruptly.

Sadi had a perfect eye for faces and ear for names. She knew these men were strangers. And somehow, Alexa, as well as Sadi, had felt that strangers meant trouble.

Alexa studied the two as she walked toward them. She could remember faces, but always forgot names. If she had to remember, she'd make up some helper like Pickle Face for a man named Heinz. Then she'd have to hope she didn't call him Mr. Claussen. No, she didn't know the detective or FBI men in the dark suit, dark shoes, and gleaming white teeth with fixed smiles.

"Alexa." Her father smiled at her, a twinkle in his eyes, as if he knew what was going on in her mind. "This is Detective Bond."

The man wore a watch that suggested he had either a wealthy wife or good instincts for investing. His name was easy. Mr. Stocks and Bonds.

He put out his hand. The one with the watch on the wrist. *He must be left-handed*, she thought.

"Go ahead, say it," Bond said. "Get it out of the way. But my first name is Norman not James." He grinned. His joke about his name and the smile took him out of the stereotype Alexa had put him into so easily.

The other detective was young. He appeared to be not much older than Alexa. But she knew it took a while to work up to detective. He, too, put out his hand. "John Blackwood. Officer Blackwood." He read her mind. "I'm with the New York City police, but I'm not a new recruit right out of the Police Academy."

Alexa felt her face flush, giving her thoughts away.

"You thought I was in high school, didn't you? Comes in handy to still look like a teenager." His eyes were chocolate brown, his hair dark brown and naturally curly. His complexion suggested, in spite of his yuppie name, that he was part Hispanic.

"Alexa, sit down," her father suggested. "I think you'll find this interesting. These men have a tempting job offer for me and another for you."

"A job for me?" Now Alexa was really puzzled, but intrigued, she'd admit. Could they get her on a fast track to the police academy or FBI? That was her career goal, but she lamented the fact that it would take so long to get qualified and trained.

"Crime among and against young people has stepped way up in the last five years," Detective Bond said. "The Lexie Talbott case has brought this to our attention again. In brainstorming what we could do about it, John had a bold suggestion." Bond nodded to Officer Blackwood to take over.

"I'm a lot older than I look." He smiled at Alexa again. "But looking like a kid, and with a little work, a punk kid, allows me to mix with street gangs and keep on top of what's happening. But I need help. I've proposed that we start a new unit. We're calling it TIF, Teen Investigative Force. Our idea is to use a few real teens with special backgrounds, like you, to work for us. We'd hope the work you'd do would be fairly low key and safe, but we won't guaranteed it. The job doesn't come without risks."

"Here's where I come in, Alexa," her father said. "They want me to head up this unit. I wouldn't totally give up my private investigation business, but I'd go back to work for the police for as many hours as it takes to run this organization."

Alexa caught on. They wanted a few good Hardy Boys and Nancy Drews. But she found it hard to believe these two were asking her to work for the New York City police. "You want me on this team? I'm flattered, and it sounds exciting, but I don't think I'm qualified to do something like that."

"But you are," Blackwood said. "You've worked with your father, so you have a background in police work. You're trained in self-defense. Your father says you have good instincts, good ideas when he's brainstormed cases with you, you're confident and trustworthy—"

"Loyal, honest, a real Girl Scout." Alexa interrupted.

"Something like that. And, of course, you learn on the job." If Blackwood hadn't been older than he looked, Alexa would swear he was flirting with her. She wanted to remind him about separating business and pleasure.

"The first job we want you to take on is this," Bond said.

"We've found the high school girl, Bernadette Griffin, who sold your sister, Brianna, and Amber the Ecstacy drugs. She gave up her source, a rich kid named Marcos Pratt. That was the easy part."

"But we want to dig deeper." Blackwood handed Alexa a typed report. "We think someone is specifically targeting high school kids and selling them Ecstasy. It's big business. We want to know who that guy is. Who is heading up this drug distribution center."

"I—I—"Alexa fumbled with the paperwork, pretending to read it.

"You don't have to decide tonight. Think this over, Alexa. Talk with your father. He's heading up TIF, even if you say no. His job isn't contingent on your coming on board." Bond stood up to leave.

"I'll contact you tomorrow." Blackwood focused his brown eyes on hers, a serious look on his face. "And if you see me hanging out at your school, you don't know me."

As soon as they were gone, her father wheeled his chair around, and rolled into the kitchen area. He poured Alexa a cup of coffee, and brought it back to where she sat, stunned with this idea.

"The job might be dangerous, Alexa. Drug dealers make big money. They don't want anyone messing with their distribution."

"It could have been Emma."

"What?"

"Emma could have been the one who died, Dad."

"I've thought of that. I don't think I can take another loss. I have mixed emotions about your working undercover for the police. I couldn't handle anything happening to you."

"You put your life at risk every time you put on your uniform, Dad. You never said that, but as soon as we were old enough to understand, we knew the danger of your being a cop. Mom knew it."

"She never once complained. Never once did she ask me to do anything else."

"You were a cop when you met." Alexa stirred cream into her

coffee until it was the caramel color she liked.

"And she was a court reporter. She listened to crime stories every day. Real ones, not the ones on TV where the bad guy always gets caught."

"Okay, what are we going to do first?" Alexa sipped her coffee. She didn't really have to make a decision. The job appealed to her. Someone supplying her sister with drugs made her angry. Emma was never going to get over losing Lexie and feeling as if it was her fault.

"Where's Emma?" Alexa jumped up. She hadn't seen Emma all day.

"I haven't seen her today. I stayed up reading half the night, then slept in. You didn't see her this morning?"

"No." Alexa ran to her sister's room, knocked, then went in.

The place was empty. Emma's bed was perfectly made up, piled with pillows and stuffed animals. One of the animals uncurled, sat up, and yawned. Rags, the rag doll Siamese that Alexa had given Emma for her birthday, would have been camouflaged if she hadn't moved.

"Hi, Rags." Alexa bent to give the soft, friendly cat a tummy rub. "Seen Emma?"

Had Emma slept there last night? Alexa realized she didn't know. Then she realized she rarely knew where Emma was, how she was spending her time, with whom. Emma had become so difficult to be around, Alexa had left her alone. Too often alone.

She had no problem with snooping. Emma's computer was dark on her desk. The desk was organized, clean. Too clean for a fifteen-year-old girl, but then, Emma had always been a neat freak. By her bed with its pink flowered spread, on the bed table rested a fat book.

Alexa looked at the title. "Les Miserables." Was Emma reading this? The book fell open at the marker. To Alexa's surprise the book was in French, and Emma appeared to be about halfway though. Her sister, the one who pretended to be the model for all the blonde jokes was reading "Les Mis" in French?

No cell, of course. Emma would have her phone with her. But there was a small date book on the back of Emma's desk. Alexa popped it open, then dug in her pocket for her own cell. She dialed Emma. No answer. Then she dialed Amber Quint. A female answered.

"Mrs. Quint, this is Alexa Kane. Is my sister, Emma, there?"

"No, and neither is Amber. She's supposed to be grounded, but you know how that goes. If you find them, will you tell Amber to check in with me? We're going out for dinner, but wanted to tell Amber to meet us. How's Emma doing?"

"Not good. I hear her crying at night."

"None of them will ever get over this. Do the police know who sold the girls drugs?"

Alexa didn't think that information was a secret. "Yes, they have them in custody."

"Good. Have you tried Brianna's house? The girls like it there because Mrs. Sasa works till six."

"Do you have an address for the Sasas?" Alexa decided to see where the girls like to hang out.

With the information in hand, Alexa took off, leaving her father on the phone. She mouthed "Be right back" and he nodded.

The Sasa address was too far to walk. Alexa called a cab and asked the dispatcher if Ralph was available. "Sure is, Miss. I'll call him." The cabbie was her father's friend, another former police officer on disability, Ralph Dunlap. When Ralph stopped at her curb, she jumped in the front passenger seat and gave him Brianna's address.

"Slumming?" Ralph asked with a grin.

Ralph was a rumpled, disheveled version of Colombo without the raincoat. He came across as clueless, but Alexa happened to know he was street smart, observant, and had a fine eye for detail. As a cop, he had been on the street, but if he had worked undercover, he'd be able to find out most anything you wanted to know.

He was a good driver and had driven a cab in Manhattan since he left police work. He said he had taken "an easy job." Anyone, however, who thought driving a cab in New York was a piece of cake should try it for a couple of days. The cabbies were treated as if they were invisible, susceptible to robbery, and their driving skills were taken for granted. But Alexa noticed that Ralph never complained. Most of the time, he seemed to be having fun outwitting frustrated drivers.

"Yeah." She answered his question. "We've lost Emma, who's supposed to be grounded, but you probably know how that is. I think she's with her friends, but I want to make sure."

Ralph zipped down back streets quickly, avoiding rush hour traffic, to get Alexa to the West Village.

"Thanks, Ralph," Alexa said, handing him the fare plus a small tip. Her budget was stretched thin and the month had hardly begun.

The Sasas lived in a renovated brownstone, similar to the Talbotts'. How did Emma keep up with these girls? For that matter, where did Emma get her share of the money for drugs? As soon as Emma had gotten difficult to talk to, Alexa had left her alone. Classic parent behavior from someone who never wanted to be Emma's substitute mother.

Alexa rang the bell and waited. She rang it again. The guy that finally opened the door was thin, a young Woody Allen type, complete with horn-rimmed, computer-geek glasses. He had dark hair, blue eyes, and perfect teeth. Even though he was thin, he was wearing a light blue muscle shirt, and Alexa could see that he left the computer and worked out occasionally. She fumbled for words. He stood there waiting, not helping her at all. After she was totally flustered and, for some reason, embarrassed, he grinned.

"You're selling magazines?"

"I'm sorry. I was surprised. I didn't know Brianna had an older brother, just her twin. I'm looking for the girls, specifically Emma Kane."

"Stepbrother."

"What?"

"I'm Bri's stepbrother. You know from the first marriage. Or was it the second? Let's see." He pretended to be thinking and counting off past relationships for his mother or his father. Alexa lost patience. She had no interest in his life history.

"Is Emma here?"

"Oh, yeah, and by the way, come in. Hank. My name's Hank, short for Henry." Henry suited him, but she could tell he seemed to be trying to change that image.

The house said old money. Hank didn't fit into the decor. He didn't seem comfortable in his skin or the house either. Maybe he was in between personalities.

"Nice place. Did you grow up here?" Alexa asked.

"No way. A bit over the top for my taste. I'm a new recruit, so to speak. Bad penny. Turned up here this time."

He tried to toss off the idea, but he wasn't pulling off the humorous approach. He probably didn't feel as if he belonged.

The conversation was leading nowhere. "So, where is Brianna's room? Looks like a place where a person could get lost easily."

"I drop bread crumbs." Hank grinned and led the way upstairs. At the end of a long hall, he pointed to a closed door, then turned and disappeared. Thank God.

Alexa knocked. "Emma, are you here?"

The door finally opened, letting out a cloud of sweet cigarette smoke. "What are you doing here?" Alexa asked. "Is that pot? Are you smoking pot?"

Emma looked a little lost herself, but kept her usual leave-me-alone attitude. She shrugged. "What if it is?"

"What do you mean, *what if it is*? You've just lost your best friend to drugs and here you are smoking pot? What are you thinking? And you are supposed to be grounded. You were supposed to come straight home from school. Dad was worried about you."

Emma shrugged again. "Why didn't you just call me?"

"Is your cell turned on? I tried twice."

"I have to go, Bri. See you tomorrow." Emma reached back and grabbed a small leather shoulder bag.

Amber came to the door. "I was going to get us a cab and then go on home myself, Emma."

"You're supposed to call your mother, Amber." Alexa might as well have all three girls mad at her. "Something about dinner."

"Okay, wait just a minute while I get my purse. I'll drop you both off on my way to wherever my parents are eating tonight." Amber punched a fast dial button on her cell and turned back into the room to get her things.

"We'll take our own cab." Alexa hated spending all her money on cabs, but she wanted to leave. Right now, before she strangled these three totally stupid girls. Then she had second thoughts. She pushed her way past Emma into the room.

"Before I go, while you're all together, where did you get pot? Did you buy that at the same time you bought Ecstasy?"

"We didn't buy it, Al," Emma said, blinking, trying to focus and clear her head. "Lexie did. She gave us all some. I let Bri keep mine here, since you like snooping through my room all the time."

"How long have you been smoking?" Alexa's anger was dissipating, and she found that a helpless feeling was taking its place.

Emma shrugged. "Not long. We just thought we'd try it. It's no big deal. Lexie said everyone tries it."

Alexa had been putting a lot of blame on Emma for getting drugs for Lexie for her birthday. Suddenly she realized that Lexie was the leader of this foursome. The glue that held them together. Whatever Lexie wanted, she could persuade the other three to go along with. The other three might have physically bought the Ecstasy, but Lexie had planned it out, probably arranged the buy.

"Did Lexie get pot from Bernadette? Or was there someone besides Bernadette Griffin who was selling drugs at school?"

"Why do you want to know?" Emma's defenses flew in place again.

"I just wondered if you asked anyone else. How'd you find out who to ask, where to get something?"

Now Amber shrugged. "Everyone knows. Lexie just asked some of the popular kids. Did the cops arrest Bernadette for dealing?"

Alexa stared at the trio of friends who were trying to be cool. And who were now trying to drown their grief at losing Lexie with smoking a different, a safer, they thought, drug. They didn't meet her eyes. "Yes, and they arrested the guy who supplied her. Did they get the right people?"

"We don't know, Al," Emma finally said. "It's not like we buy drugs every day. Just this one time." Her voice trailed off and she seemed near tears again.

Alexa put her arm around Emma and tugged her toward the stairs. "Okay, let's go home."

"Wait, I'm riding with you," Amber reminded her.

"No thanks. Stay there with Bri until you get your wits about you. Stay all night if it takes that long." It might take years, but that wasn't Alexa's worry. Emma was.

When they got outside, Al dialed the cab's number. "We have someone near you," the dispatcher told her. "The same one you rode with earlier. He'll be there in a jiffy."

Ralph was cruising the neighborhood, Alexa guessed, looking for a fare back to SoHo. Or looking after her, as he had a tendency to do. She knew Ralph did that as a favor to her father. "I was hoping you'd need to go back," Ralph said, smiling at Alexa and Emma in the rearview mirror.

"Thanks, Ralph," Alexa said.

My God, if she was going to work undercover, she'd gotten a bad start on the job. Every guy she'd met tonight memorized how she looked, not to mention flirted with her. Ralph was always a flirt, a harmless flirt, since then he turned around and talked about his wife. They'd been together over forty years.

But Hank Sasa. She didn't have him figured out by a long shot. He seemed older than high school. Was he in college somewhere? And why had he acted so strange and studied her so carefully? At the same time, bantering with her, teasing her.

There was no way she could make up for her lack of dating skills or the ability to read guys immediately. She hadn't resented spending all her free time at home helping take care of her mother and then working with and worrying about her father. But she wasn't shy. Maybe she had buried her intuition along with her emotions. Maybe she just needed to relax, keep her eyes and ears open.

As far as questioning the girls, she hadn't learned anything from anyone, just spent a bundle on cab fare. Maybe Emma would remember something another time and talk to her. She suspected the detective business was frustrating and occasionally boring.

"I'm sorry, Al," Emma said in a small voice. "I forgot the time. I hope Dad wasn't worried."

Well, that was something. Alone, in the back seat of Ralph's taxi, Emma turned into a real person.

"We were both worried about you, Emma." Alexa postponed the drug lecture, pulled Emma close, and sat with her arm around her little sister the whole way home.

Chapter 5

Emma went straight to her room. Alexa didn't see her again until breakfast, but she'd heard Emma throwing up in the middle of the night. Good. She hoped the pot made Emma so sick she never wanted to smoke it again.

Morning meals at the Kanes were pretty much up to each person. Usually there were bagels, cream cheese, cereal, and fruit. Their father got up early and made a big pot of coffee, then went to the police gym to work out.

"Emma, what do you know about Brianna's stepbrother?" Alexa asked, hoping that was a safe question. She was so glad to see Emma in the kitchen, and without a scowl, she didn't want to upset her.

"He's a snoop. Bri hates him." Emma bit into a cinnamon raisin bagel smeared with cream cheese and strawberry jam. She licked her fingers where the jam oozed over. Today she was wearing jeans and a pink T-shirt that actually came to her belt line. She had tied a colorful woven pink and purple belt in the loops. In her ears were what looked like Alexa's big gold hoops, but Alexa didn't say anything. Emma looked really cute.

"He acted as if he hadn't been there long." Alexa sipped her coffee au lait, feeling the caffeine send a much-needed buzz to her brain. She hadn't slept well, dreaming of fighting off men in black hoods who kept coming as fast as she could knock them down.

"He hasn't. About a couple of weeks, I guess. Something about his mother remarrying and not wanting him around. Bri said it was the second time this happened."

"That can't be very good for his ego." Alexa decided her shredded wheat biscuits had soaked long enough so she dropped in a handful of blueberries and took a bite.

"You think Dad will ever marry again?" Emma didn't look at Alexa when she asked that question.

"I doubt it, Em. He and Mom were so much in love. Remember that night we sneaked out of bed to watch them dancing in the living room. And how Dad always brought her those bouquets of flowers, the kind she carried in her bridal bouquet? That kind of perfect love usually doesn't happen twice. We'd be lucky if that happened to us, that we found some guy who was a perfect soul mate."

Alexa had such wonderful memories of her mother and father together. She tried not to let them make her feel sad, but glad they had as much time as they did together.

"Do you like Peter?"

"I guess so. He's nice enough. We didn't have much time to talk before—"

"Yeah, I know. I gotta go." Emma jumped up and grabbed her book bag. "Where's Sadi?"

"I was wondering that myself. She's usually here by now. I'll wait a few more minutes." Alexa glanced at her cell phone. No calls.

Their father came in just as Emma left. "Emma eat breakfast?"

"Yes, for a change. I think my coming after her last night shook her up. We have to keep talking to her, Dad. Even if she won't talk to us." Alexa left out the part about finding Emma smoking pot at Bri's house. Knowing would just worry her father, and there was little he could do about it after the fact. Emma certainly knew the risks.

"I don't know what to say that I haven't already said. I did remind her that she was grounded, though. I thought Brianna and Amber were, too." Her father smeared a bagel with cream cheese.

"I get the idea that both of them pretty much take care of themselves. Mrs. Sasa said Amber was supposed to be home, but they just went on to dinner without looking for her."

Her father nodded his head and poured another cup of coffee. His T-shirt was sweat-stained, and Alexa knew he had been lifting weights this morning. He was trying to keep his upper body strong enough so he could take care of himself. It had been hard for him to accept the fact that he'd never walk again after being shot, but once he did, he adjusted and did what he needed to be independent.

Sadi burst in before they could talk more. "Sorry, Al. Hi, Tony. I got the drug lecture this morning. I was finally able to say I was going to be late for school and that's not acceptable either."

Sadi's parents had a long, unwritten list of unacceptable behavior for teens, but also for themselves. Being late for anything was way at the top of the list.

"You two better leave, Al," her father said, "but ask Sadi if she wants to be a part of TIF. We'll talk more after school."

"TIF? Is that a short version of TGIF?" Sadi asked after they were out on the street, dodging people, hurrying toward school. "OMG, it's only Tuesday. I have three tests. I'll never make it until Friday this week."

"Teen Investigative Force. It's new, Sadi. Those men in black suits last night–"

"FBI? TIF? Who were they? Cops, for sure. Not that I have anything against cops. Your dad is the nicest person I know."

"Yeah, but these guys turned out to be okay, too. They just looked intimidating. I think that's something they teach at cop school and FBI training. They want Dad to head up a new team of police." Alexa gave Sadi all the information she had so far on the new job.

"You're going to work undercover for the New York City Police Department?"

Sadi stopped dashing forward and stared at Alexa. A man nearly ran into her, but swerved, swearing under his breath.

"I haven't said yes, but it's what I want to do after I graduate from college. I'll get a head start."

"If you survive for six months. Your dad wants me on this team, too?" Sadi looked serious for a minute. "If you're going to do it, I'd like to, but you know my parents. If they have to sign anything, there's no way."

"I'm sure they'd have to give permission. Maybe you can just help me on the side, you know, look up people on the computer, find out stuff."

"The boring work."

"Yeah, while I'm out kicking butt."

They had to run to get to class, so the discussion was postponed. But it was all Alexa could think about all day. Then at noon, she got a phone call. A number she didn't recognize.

"Yes?"

"Blackwood here, Alexa. You'll know my number now, right?"

"Are you going to call me all the time?"

"Probably." She could hear the smile in his voice. "I got you an appointment to talk to Bernadette Griffin after school. Can you come uptown?"

"This is going to interfere with my love life, isn't it?"

"You have one?"

"No, but maybe I'm open to the idea. A guy will freak out if I say, let me check with my police contact."

"You're smart. You'll think of something. See you around four."

She had a Tae Kwon Do class and three exams this week, but she wanted this job. She'd juggle her time to keep up. She wanted to find out who was supplying ninth graders with drugs.

After school she told Sadi to make an excuse for her with Mr. Chee, to say she'd make up today's class another time. She swung onto the bus to go to the police station, feeling as if she had a sign on her back that said, Working Undercover Now. She'd stopped being good at pretending once she and Sadi and Emma had stopped raiding her mother's closet. Acting wasn't a skill you could pick up overnight.

She had her phone on vibrate, and when it went off, it got her attention. But this time there was a text message.

DO YOU REALLY WANT TO DO THIS?

No name, no number. No way to trace who'd sent it.

She looked around inside the crowded bus. Right behind her were two little old ladies chatting about some celebrity they'd seen while they were having lunch. There were two tired-looking secretary types. A really gorgeous blonde carried a portfolio with a look that said rejection. "Sorry, wrong type. Try us again sometime." Two construction workers who looked exhausted slumped in their seats and weren't talking at all. No one looked at her. No one looked familiar. Certainly, no one knew what she was doing, where she was going. No one cared, either. Everyone was tied up in his or her own little world.

How much paranoia came with this job? She was not a fearful person. But a vibration, not unlike her cell phone, started in her stomach and pounded its way up into her chest.

Chapter 6

ait a minute. She hadn't known she was coming uptown until Blackwood called her. Who had she told? Sadi. She shrugged, pulled out her calculus book and tried to study for a few minutes. Her brain was on pulse, too. She closed the book and put it in her backpack. Instead of studying, she pulled out a small notebook and made a list of things to do. Writing things down would help her think.

Interview Bernadette (a given)

Interview Marcos (ask Blackwood)

Try to buy some drugs at school, make a contact

Find out where high school people are going to party

Are there any clubs where teens can go to dance?

Maybe Peter could help out, try to score something easy like pot. She figured she had such a squeaky clean image, she might call attention to herself by asking where to buy drugs. The same went for Sadi. No one would believe Sadi was serious about wanting to alter her brain. She was so smart, it was scary.

Alexa swung off the bus and crossed the street. Why wasn't

Bernadette Griffin jailed closer to SoHo? This particular uptown precinct was in a decent neighborhood, so she didn't have to be scared.

Sidewalks were getting crowded with people coming home from work. There were a few businesses: a mom and pop grocery, a bicycle shop, a used clothing store, and seeming out of place, an elegant flower and gift shop.

A woman behind the counter inside the precinct looked at Alexa as if she was about to ask what she was doing here. "I'm here to see Officer Blackwood and a prisoner," Alexa explained, after signing her name in a register. If she was working undercover, should she sign her real name?

John Blackwood came out to get her. "Hi, Alexa. Glad you could come. Did you check in?"

"Yes, I wondered if I should have used my real name. What does working undercover mean? Am I supposed to keep it a secret that I'm talking to Bernadette?"

Blackwood grinned. "Well, nothing is too hush-hush yet. Just best not to tell many people what you're doing."

Alexa hesitated. "Someone already knows, who seems to think I'm doing the wrong thing. But I have no idea who sent me the text message."

Blackwood frowned. "Let me know if it happens again." He opened a file folder he carried and took out two laminated cards that looked similar to a driver's license. He handed them to Alexa. "Before I forget it, Alexa, I took the liberty of getting you and your friend Sadi new IDs. They say you're twenty-one."

"Can I pass for twenty-one?" Alexa took the card and studied it. Blackwood had taken a photo she'd given her dad to make the cards.

"Use more makeup. Smile a lot. Dress sexy. Look sexy. No one checks the photo as much as they do the birthday, your age."

"If you say so." Alexa took the two cards and buttoned them into the pocket of her cargo pants.

"In addition, I had one of our staff make you up a lipstick." He handed a silver tube to Alexa. "Pink. Your favorite color."

Alexa was too surprised to speak, but she felt her cheeks grow hot.

"We're trained to be observant." Blackwood smiled. "Twist the bottom ring you get lipstick. Twist the second ring you turn on a tracking device."

Alexa laughed. "A James-Bond toy."

"We do have them. Someone in our computer department will be alerted if you activate this and will track where you are. Don't wait until you're in trouble to use it."

"Do you expect me to get in trouble?" Alexa had to ask.

"We all do occasionally. Part of the job." Now Blackwood didn't smile. "We hope you won't need to call for help, but don't hesitate. Don't try to be a hero."

You can count on that, Alexa thought, looking over the silver tube, but being careful not to turn it on.

Blackwood led her through several doors to the back of the building. Then he left her alone in a small room with a one-way window. The light was dim and the room smelled of stale cigarette smoke and cleaning disinfectant. Alexa's skin prickled. She imagined ghosts of all the prisoners who'd sat in this room, denying guilt for anything.

Bernadette came into the room slowly, giving Alexa a curious stare. She sat across from Al. "What do you want?"

Bernadette Griffin was a sad-looking girl trying to be tough. She wore her bleached blonde hair butch, had a tattoo bracelet around her left wrist, a tiny rose tattoo on her shoulder, and a barbed-wire tattoo necklace tight around her neck. The sleeves were cut out of her T-shirt and left ragged. Her jeans were actually in fashion with torn knees and ragged cuffs—except that rich kids wearing stressed jeans had paid a hundred dollars a pair, and Bernadette's were probably from Target and then legitimately worn out.

Her eyes were light brown, tired with dark circles and red as if she'd been crying.

"You know who I am, Bernadette?"

"I've seen you around. You don't usually speak to people like me. Now not even my father will speak to me."

"Has he been to visit you here?"

"Sent his lawyer with a message that he was pissed off and disappointed. What else is new?"

"You don't get along with him?"

"Why should I?"

"Girls usually get along with fathers better than mothers."

"That the case at your house?"

Alexa didn't want to share her life story with Bernadette. "Yeah. My dad's cool." Alexa let a minute go by before saying anything else.

"Why were you selling drugs? Did you just want the money for clothes and stuff?"

"Something like that. Money gets you noticed. Makes you popular."

Bernadette seemed to think that money was key to being happy. "Is Marcos rich?" Alexa asked.

Bernadette shrugged. "I guess. He's got a nice ride, buys anything he wants."

"He's your main crush?" Alexa tried making statements rather than outright questions. If she could get Bernadette in a friendly conversation, she might get more information.

"I guess. Is he in jail?"

"You told the police who he was, didn't you?"

"No, I've kept my mouth shut. If he's in jail, someone else ratted on him." Bernadette looked down at blue fingernails, paint chipped, ends nibbled to the quick.

"How'd you meet him?"

"He offered me a ride home one day. It was raining. I figured what the hell, he looked safe."

"You hadn't known him before?"

"He didn't go to Stuyvesant. Said he graduated a couple of years ago and was working."

"Did he say where he was working?"

"No. Didn't matter. He took me out for a burger before he dropped me off home. Then when he saw where I lived, I guess he was impressed. He asked if he could see me again."

"Where do you live?"

"Central Park West. Tony part of town, right? I **didn't** care if he thought I was rich. He did hand me some smokes before I got out of the car, then grinned."

"Pot?"

"Yeah. I'd never smoked it, but when I did, I liked it. Made everything go away and my dad angry." She shrugged. "I liked that, too."

"Marcos ever say where he got his supplies?"

"No, and I didn't ask."

"So you started selling in school for him?"

"Not until those ninth graders asked me if I could get them something. Seemed easy enough and they begged me."

Alexa hated the image of Emma, Amber and Bri begging Bernadette to get them Ecstasy. "How'd they know to ask you?"

"I don't know."

"I think you're lying. I think lots of people knew to come to you. Marcos got you hooked so you would deal for him."

"Who are you?" As if Bernadette has just woken up, she sat up straighter, looked at Alexa, and questioned her being there.

"You supplied drugs to my sister, who gave them to her friend. That friend, Bernadette, is now dead. Do you feel any responsibility for that?"

Bernadette shrugged, but had the decency to look down and lose the defiance she'd shown.

Alexa didn't think she was going to get any more information, so she stood up and knocked on the door for the guard to let her out.

Blackwood was waiting in the hall. He had been watching the interview through the one-way window into the room. "Any luck?"

"I don't think she knows anything. Marcos got her addicted and kept her that way by making her deal for him in the high school. She's trying to look and be tough, but she's not very good at it."

"That was pretty much my take on her. She wanted to be popular, and she took this route. Her father is a fairly well-known business man. Not extremely wealthy, but not hurting for money, either. His wife left him when Bernadette was twelve, just disappeared,. Left a note saying she was tired of being married and tired of being a mother. I guess she calls Bernadette a couple of times a year, but Bernadette won't talk to her."

"If you're trying to get me to feel sorry for her, I don't." A sudden flash of anger came over Alexa.

"I know. It's okay. We all have problems, but fortunately, we don't all use them as an excuse to fail."

"Do weekly lectures go with this job?" Alexa backed off on turning her anger toward Blackwood.

"Depends. Anger and frustration come free, too. Want a ride home?"

"Can I turn on the siren?"

"My ride is unmarked." Blackwood grinned.

"Unless you feel like setting one of those little lights on top and chasing after someone."

"You watch too much TV."

"Everything I know about crime I learned from the tube."

"With your dad one of the best cops in the city? I don't buy that."

"Yeah, he was," Alexa said, feeling a flash of sadness for her dad. "The best."

Alexa remembered how handsome her dad looked every time he left the house or returned in his uniform. She never thought to worry about him. She never thought about the possibility of his being hurt or killed.

Her mother was surely responsible for Alexa's peace of mind. Mom never once seemed to worry, or if she did, she worried in secret.

Alexa missed her mother. But she wasn't as lost as Bernadette.

Imagine a woman saying, "I don't want to be your mother anymore," then disappearing. That was as bad as Bri's mother saying, "Go away, I have a new husband and no time for a teenaged son."

Alexa was going right home and thank her father for being such a great person.

Chapter 7

Alexa had wanted to talk to her dad when she got home, but he was gone. She remembered tonight was his poker night. He wouldn't be home until late.

She searched in the kitchen, heated some leftover pasta, and took it to her room to eat while she made some lists. What had she learned today? Not much, except that in wanting to be popular, Bernadette had made some bad choices. Being popular was overrated, she thought, and it didn't always last. She was afraid Emma was setting herself up for the same trap.

Emma had friends, but Alexa knew she felt insecure. If she had been stronger, she'd have suggested some other gift for Lexie. Emma was a follower, and Alexa didn't know anything she could do about it. Losing their mother had been devastating for both of them, but Alexa didn't think Emma had made much progress at healing. And now she had another death to deal with.

She had finished her dinner and was staring at a calculus problem when her phone rang. She checked the number, but it wasn't familiar.

"Hello?"

"Al, you studying?" The deep voice sending shivers through her whole body belonged to Peter Talbott.

"Pretending to be. I don't know why I took so much math and science this year. Did you have Franklin for calculus?"

"Franklinstein? Yeah, he's hard. Never explains much, expects you to understand it by osmosis. Need some help?"

Alexa hesitated. Would she get any studying done if she let Peter come and pretend to help her? Did she care? She wanted to see him again.

Peter took advantage of her silence. "Or, here's another plan. I know where a party is going to be hot. I can pick you up. We can drop in and see who's there."

"You want me to just give up on studying and go to a party?"

"Seems like a good idea. You probably think it would be more fitting for me to sit home and grieve for Lexie. But I'm alone here, Al, and going a little bit nuts, stir crazy. I loved Lexie. I don't need any rules about how to handle losing her."

"I didn't mean it that way, Peter." Alexa understood what Peter was saying. After her mother died, people seemed eager to tell both Alexa and Emma how to act, how to feel. "She's in a better place." "It was the Lord's will." "Time will heal." None of the platitudes helped Alexa heal in the slightest, and some of the things people said upset her. There was no better place for her mother, no place she'd rather be, than right here with her family. Alexa truly thought God's will was perfect health and happiness. She knew people meant well, but Peter was right. No one can tell you how to feel, how to grieve, what is proper behavior, when someone you love dies.

"I know you didn't. I was just hoping to see you tonight."

Peter's voice was persuasive. One of Alexa's plans was to find some parties to check out. If Lexie's party was any indication, there were always drugs at parties, and where better for someone who was dealing to make contacts? There were a dozen reasons why she should stay home and do her homework. She hated parties. But she'd put parties on her list of things to do. Parties were work. You didn't always get to do what you liked when you were a spy. She could use some dating experience. She liked Peter. A lot. Alexa grinned and was glad Peter couldn't see her going over all her options.

"Okay, let's go out. I can do some research."

"Research?" He took two beats to wonder what Alexa meant, but he didn't ask. "If you say so. Be there in half an hour."

At least he wasn't outside her door using a cell phone. Alexa scrambled to dress a little more like a party, although school clothes would have been all right. Maybe she was dressing up for Peter. *Don't go there.* Of course, she was dressing up for Peter.

She pulled on some white cotton capri pants, and, taking a lesson from Emma, threaded a burgundy and black print chiffon scarf through the belt loops. A black tank would match. She pulled her hair up into a knot and wished she had the big, thin hoop earrings Emma had borrowed. Tiny silver rings would have to do. Just a flick of eye shadow and mascara, pink lipstick, and she was ready to roll. She searched in a drawer. The pants were so tight they were made without pockets. She needed a small purse. Normally, she hated carrying anything, but—

Emma had a drawer full of accessories. She hurried out and knocked on Emma's door. No answer. She hesitated, then opened her door. "Hi, Rags."

The ragdoll Siamese looked up at her, stretched, and yawned. Where was Emma? Grounded meant nothing to her. Alexa looked at the dresser Emma had painted, each drawer a different color. Pink for accessories? The drawer was small. Alexa pulled it open. Bingo.

A stack of small purses gave her a choice. She tugged at a small black leather bag with a long thin shoulder strap.

As Alexa pulled out the purse, untangled it from others, a scrap of paper rose to the surface. Too tempting. Two scribbled names: Bernadette Griffin. Billy Razzi. Alexa tucked the paper into the black purse, closed the drawer quietly, then hurried back to her own room.

Into the purse she tossed her cell phone, a tissue, her own tube of pink lipstick–not the new toy—, a pen, and a tiny notebook. Five dollars mad money. Would that get a taxi home? She didn't plan on having a fight with Peter, but a girl had to be ready to be independent. She searched for four quarters.

She ran to the door when Peter knocked and pulled it open.

"Wow, that's what I like—a girl who's eager." Peter smiled and Alexa took a deep breath.

"How about on time? Or, I could admit, I'm eager to leave the calculus and worry about it tomorrow."

"You sure know how to flatter a guy." Peter flashed his thousand-watt smile and led the way to the elevator.

"Is your ego that shaky?" Alexa asked when Peter took her hand and headed for the subway entrance.

"Oh yeah. I'm not as popular as rumor would have it."

"True confessions. Hummm. Sadi helps me with all my math and science classes."

"I like you, Al. I wish we'd met some other way."

"Yeah, me, too."

They were quiet for a few minutes after the subway car came and they got seated. The silence had a quality of sadness, but wasn't uncomfortable. Alexa leaned back, closed her eyes, and let a wave of sorrow move through her entire body. She felt exhausted and wondered if going out was a good decision after all. She hated to be poor company. She made a decision.

"Peter, while we're at this party, I need some help."

"What kind? A dance lesson? I know you don't need pool lessons. How about ping-pong?"

"More serious than that. I'm trying to find out who else might be dealing drugs in the high school. If you see any obvious exchange of money and drugs, would you let me know?"

"Okay. But what are you going to do? Ask for the seller's name?"

"I'd hope not to be that obvious. You point someone out, I'll get his or her name."

"Alexa Kane, girl spy."

"Do you always make fun of your dates?"

"Only when they're so mysterious."

For some reason Alexa didn't tell Peter about her truly being a kind of spy. She figured she could trust him, but if undercover was to mean anything, the fewer people who knew what she was doing, the better. She might need more help from Peter later, and she wouldn't hesitate to ask him, but for now, she'd just pretend to be curious.

They walked a few blocks in a part of the city unfamiliar to Alexa, but Peter seemed to know where they were going. The party scene was similar to the one for Lexie's birthday. Posh-looking house.

Dark, sweet-smelling, no parents in evidence. Thin wisps of smoke drifted from ashen corners like forgotten dreams. Girls who didn't get a Barbie for Christmas when they were eight had stopped believing in Santa, stopped believing what parents said, stopped caring about themselves. Boys felt powerful after the first puff from a joint, were sure they were Brad Pitt after the second.

"How do you find out about these parties?" Alexa whispered, as if the information might be a secret.

"Ask around. Word travels from person to person."

"So not everyone here was invited?"

"Maybe only half were invited. Half, like us, are crashing."

As Alexa looked around, people looked older than at Lexie's party, but she didn't recognize anyone. The music was loud downstairs. No one seemed to be talking anyway. They were laughing, giggling, or saying things like, "Yeah, man." "Go for it." "Hey, Dude, share."

Her eyes started to water, and Alexa headed for a room that wasn't so smoky. Downstairs, a rec room had been cleared for a dance floor. The music was slow and seductive. Couples moved as one, slowly, not speaking.

"Dance?" Peter held out his arms. Alexa stepped into them, but kept her distance. She did like to dance, but she felt shivery so close to him.

"Scared of me?"

"Yes." She leaned in a little, resting her head on his shoulder.

"Happens to me all the time. I'm going to have to get counseling."

She smiled, but, of course, he couldn't see. "Counseling is good. Never know what kind of hidden problems you may have."

"I only date girls who have black belts. Then I feel safe all evening."

"But do they?"

"Unfortunately, they probably do."

The music stopped, and they wandered around looking for something to drink. In the kitchen, tubs of ice offered soft drinks. A pile of sandwiches filled one tray. All sorts of pastries were heaped on another. A birthday sheet cake with frosted sentiments but no candles had only a couple of slices missing. *Happy 18th Birthday, Roxanne.* Where was Roxanne?

"Bring your own beer." Peter reached in the tub and pulled out two Cokes. "This okay?"

"You didn't bring beer?" Alexa was teasing, but he took it seriously.

"I don't drink."

"Reason for that?"

"Yes."

She waited but he walked out of the kitchen, guessing she would follow. Quietly, they walked all over the house. Peter seemed curious, and she was, too, of course. If anyone had hard drugs, they didn't take them in public. If anyone had anything for sale, it wasn't obvious, either.

Back at the dance, the music was faster and more people were moving around the floor. Alexa felt comfortable dancing farther from Peter. She liked looking at his smiling face and his brown eyes that said he was having fun.

But someone else apparently wanted to dance close. They changed the CD. A slow fifties piece that Alexa recognized from her dad's extensive record collection sent her into Peter's arms again. Looking over his shoulder, she spotted a guy in the corner staring at her. The light was dim enough that she didn't recognize him. But she didn't think she knew him anyway.

"You aren't giving me your full attention, are you?" Peter whispered, his breath warm on her ear. She shivered.

"Sorry. I'll try harder. She snuggled close and decided she didn't care who was watching.

Just as the number stopped, and Peter pushed her away slightly, and she thought he might be going to kiss her, all hell broke loose.

"Police!" someone yelled. "Police, get outta here."

"Great," Alexa said under her breath. "Just what I needed. Do you think there's a back way out of here?"

"We can try. I don't need another arrest on my rap sheet." Peter grabbed her arm and moved in the opposite direction from the crowd. People separated, making a path for them.

"Are you ever serious about anything, Peter?"

"Or anyone? Sometimes."

She didn't have to look at him to know he was smiling as they slipped into the cool, welcome outside air. Honeysuckle scent perfumed the tiny back patio. She glanced around. The small square of flagstone was enclosed with a high wall. No way out. Could they just hide for a few minutes?

Alexa took a deep breath and thought about what she'd learned inside. Only that Peter seemed to like her a lot and that she felt really comfortable with him.

She didn't tell him that. Telling a guy you were comfortable with him was probably akin to telling him he was boring. Peter Talbott was far from boring.

Chapter 8

People came to the back door, saw it was a dead end, whirled around, and headed for the front of the house. For a couple of minutes, Alexa and Peter waited for the crowd to leave. Then they made their way back to the only way out. People were exiting the house like rats leaving the proverbial ship. Some were jumping over small hedges, some stomping through flower beds, giggling and calling to each other, running down the streets to find transportation.

Had a neighbor reported the noise? Or had someone in the house called it in, possibly even the person living there who saw her party getting out of hand? Happy Birthday, Roxanne. Sorry to spoil your day.

"The nearest subway is two blocks away," Peter said. "Should we run or pretend we live in this neighborhood and are out for a stroll?"

Once Alexa got over her initial moment of fear and surprise, she saw this as an adventure. She took Peter's hand and pulled him out to the street. "I don't think we can be arrested for being at a party." But I'm not sure, she added to herself.

A young woman stood at the front curb in an explaining pose, crying and talking to police.

Alexa ran right into a uniform. In the dim light from street lamps and flashlights, she looked down at highly polished black shoes. Uh-oh. She looked up at Officer Blackwood.

"Alexa? What are you doing here?" His face was as stormy as the night was clear and cloudless.

Alexa shrugged and said the first thing that came to her mind. "Research?" Then she giggled, under the influence of nothing but Coke and embarrassment.

Blackwood sighed and looked at Peter. "You taking her home?"

"Yes, sir." Peter was extra polite.

"Get her out of here."

"Gladly." Peter grabbed Alexa's hand.

Leaving, she looked around again, even though it was dark on the sidewalk. But there was just enough light from the street lamp to see a guy leaning on a tree trunk, watching the chaos. It was the guy who'd been watching her dance. He smiled at her, waved, then faded into the shadows.

Alexa shivered, not understanding her reaction, but not liking it either. Had he been watching her all evening?

"Good thing you're friends with a lot of cops." Peter said, walking fast, hurrying to get a subway train that would return them to SoHo.

"Yeah, that was a friend of my dad's. It would have been really embarrassing to have my father come and bail me out of jail. Maybe I'd have told him to leave you there."

"Hey, this is not my fault. Weren't you having fun until the raid?" There was laughter in Peter's voice.

"Some. Who do you think called the police?"

"Could have been anyone. But my money is on a neighbor."

Riding back across town, Alexa debated telling Peter about TIF. Something held her back. The fewer people who knew about the new organization, the better. If she really, seriously needed Peter's help with something, she'd tell him then. It wasn't her place to recruit people to join the unit.

Peter walked her to the door and would probably have kissed her goodnight, but Alexa's emotions were already in a whirl.

"Goodnight. Fun evening, I guess." She laughed, unlocked the entry door of their building, and slipped inside. She did turn back to wave and to see that Peter was grinning. She hadn't hurt his feelings.

She wasn't a person to hurry any kind of a relationship. There was Sadi, who'd been in her life since they were kids. But who else was close to her? Her father and Emma. What did that tell her? Well, she didn't trust easily, and she was busy, too busy for clubs or anything casual.

Is Peter going to become something more than casual? A little voice argued with her. *You know you like him a lot.* "Hey, I don't know." She didn't realize she had spoken aloud until her father spoke to her.

"Alexa, is that you?" Her father was still up, looking at his computer screen, his back to her.

"Is Emma home?" Alexa asked first.

"She's been home all evening as far as I know. Is it natural for a fifteen-year-old girl to live in her room?"

"When she's not in her friends' rooms, yes." Alexa walked quietly to Emma's door, listened, slipped the door open, and peeked in. Emma and Rags were curled together. Neither woke. Alexa realized she wanted to turn a key and keep Emma there for at least two years. She knew that was unrealistic. Her major role was going to become that of a mother. Worrying.

"You and Sadi go to a movie?" Her father asked, shutting off his computer.

Alexa and Sadi almost never went to a movie in a theater. Dad knew that. She answered his real question. "Peter Talbott and I went to a party. The cops raided it."

"It would have been embarrassing to come to the station to bail you out, Al." Was her father teasing or scolding? Sometimes his voice was so controlled, Alexa wasn't sure.

"Dad, the entire house was full of people smoking pot and drinking. If there was any other drug available, I didn't see it. But I'm sure there was."

"Did you see anyone handing stuff out?"

"No, that's what I was watching for, but I'm sure someone dealing would be really careful. They'd probably go into a bathroom or bedroom and close the door." She thought of the guy who kept watching her. "Is TIF just getting started, or would you have someone already working undercover, going to parties, places where teens congregate?"

"As far as I know, TIF is a new idea. I don't have anyone else working. That's not to say the police don't have men or women who look really young slipping into the teen scene just to keep them in touch with that age group."

"There was a guy at the party who kept watching me."

"Maybe he enjoys looking at a pretty girl, a beautiful girl."

Alexa grinned. "Maybe so. I'm exhausted, Dad. If you don't hear me when you get up in the morning, will you knock on my door? I didn't get a lot of homework done tonight."

"If your grades drop, you're out."

"I figured you'd get around to saying that." Alexa slipped into her room, out of her clothes, into a soft, but ragged nightshirt, and curled up with her own sleeping companion. She had to shove to get Black Bart to move over, then she curled around his warm body and listened to him purr for about three seconds.

Hank found Alexa the next day at school. She and Sadi had just separated and headed for their first class.

"Alexa, did you learn anything new?" He studied her from behind his horn-rimmed glasses.

"I beg your pardon?"

"Yesterday, at the police station. Didn't you go there to see Bernadette? What did you find out that the police didn't already know?"

"Are you following me, Hank?" Alexa stopped abruptly at the door of her English class. "Are you the one who called me?"

"I just happened to see you go in there. What else would you have been doing?"

"And how did you just happen to be all the way uptown at the same time that I was?"

"Coincidence?" Hank stared at her with his intense blue eyes, his unnerving stare. Alexa had to look away.

"Did you call me?"

"Yeah, your dad answered. If a parent answers, hang up."

She meant on her cell. But how would Hank get her cell phone number? Would Emma give it to him? She might if he asked for it. Alexa made a mental note to ask Emma.

"Leave me alone, Hank." Alexa stepped into the classroom and slid into her seat.

It took a few moments before she heard anything her political science teacher said. And this was another class to which she needed to pay close attention. If she was going to flunk a class, it was calculus, but she didn't have any easy classes this year. She needed a high GPA to get into college, then see if she could get into the FBI program.

But she couldn't get the party with the mysterious stranger, Hank, and Peter out of her mind. Had she suddenly become a hottie, all these guys watching her, calling her, flirting? She didn't think so. Did one of them have a reason for wanting to know where she went, who she was with, and to be the first to know if she found out anything that would help the police? That was a more likely scenario. She was supposed to be weaving a web to pull in a criminal. But it felt more like she was becoming entangled in the web herself.

Chapter 9

Alexa had tucked the scrap of paper where Emma had scribbled both Bernadette Griffin's and Billy Razzi's names into her pocket. On her free period she stopped at the office.

"Hi, Ms. Stanford," she said to the school secretary. "How can I find out what period Billy Razzi is in right now?"

"We don't usually give out that information, Alexa." Mrs. Stanford was a fixture at Stuyvesant, tough, and strict with rules. "Why did you need to know?" She looked at Alexa and frowned.

When all else fails, tell the truth. Alexa looked around, leaned in close. "Well, the truth is, Ms. Stanford, I got his name from my sister Emma after Lexie Talbott died of a drug overdose." She didn't hesitate to play the sympathy card, either. Whatever got her information. "I have reason to believe that Billy might also be dealing drugs here. But don't tell anyone I told you that, since I have no evidence whatsoever, and I wouldn't want to ruin his reputation if that's not the case."

Ms. Stanford's gray eyes flew wide open behind her wire-rimmed glasses. She stared at Alexa for a minute. "Billy Razzi has been in here several times to talk to the principal, but I didn't realize he was that much of a troublemaker. His problems are usually missing too many classes and failing grades."

Stanford didn't even realize she was giving out other confidential information. Alexa didn't let on. Being a troublemaker, and skipping classes didn't make someone a criminal. All that was usual teen behavior for anyone with an attitude problem.

Without saying more, the secretary looked in a file, slipped a page into a copier, then handed Alexa Billy Razzi's entire daily schedule. "I have no idea how you got this information, Alexa."

"Deal. Thanks." The paper, folded, disappeared into one of the many pockets in Alexa's cargo pants.

She stopped in the restroom, went into a stall, dug the schedule out, and memorized the next three hours of Billy's life. How was she going to know which guy he was?

Spending a half hour in the library, the room closest to Billy's English classroom, she left just before the buzzer announced a class change. In the hall, she leaned on the wall and pretended to be reading as people filed out and hurried away.

"Looking for me?" A voice made her look up quickly. Standing in front of her, way too close, was the guy who was watching her at last night's party. He wasn't tall, no taller than Alexa, but he oozed with animal magnetism and confidence. Even with him wearing a long sleeve white shirt and a suit jacket, Alexa could see that he lifted weights. He probably spent more time in the gym than Alexa did at her Tae Kwon Do classes. His eyes were green, sparkling with laughter because of catching Alexa spying on him. They were even.

"Huh? No. What makes you think that?"

"Call it an educated guess. You're supposed to be in the science wing right now, aren't you?" He grinned at Alexa, a sassy, smart-aleck grin. She wanted to take off and totally ignore him.

"This is my free period. How do you know my schedule?"

"You seem to know mine."

"I—I heard you were selling. That true?"

"Why would you think I was selling anything?"

"You were at the party last night. Looked to me like everyone there was either selling or buying. I have a fifty-fifty chance of your having something I want."

Billy liked the double meaning of that phrase way too much. He kept staring at her until she wanted to wipe the cocky grin off his face and give up this attempt at catching him with pot or anything else.

"Tell you what? You go with me tonight and I'll get you whatever you need, maybe even more. Bring cash. I don't take credit cards."

"I have to go out with you to get some weed?"

"I'm fresh out." He pulled out an empty pants pocket to make his point. "And besides, you think I'd just walk around this place with my pockets full of brain-candy? They have my number here, just because I'm a little lax about time. If I get kicked out of school, I'm in deep doo-doo. My dad's just looking for a reason to ask my mother to take me back. And she lives in Minot, North Dakota, the end of the world. Six more months I'm independent."

"A secret rendevous seems like a lot of trouble, but I'll meet you someplace." Alexa didn't know how else to find out if Billy was telling her the truth.

Billy stopped grinning and looked her over as if he could read her mind, her motives. "Nine o'clock. The Blue Orchid. It's a nightclub.

There's a rave. You'll never find me. Go up to the bar and order a Coke. I'll find you."

"You're doing what?" Sadi stared at Alexa as they started home from school.

"He said he didn't have anything on him. I didn't know any other way to find out if he was really dealing."

"And you got his name from Emma?"

"Sort of. I found this piece of paper in one of her dresser drawers. Billy's name was on it, along with Bernadette Griffin."

"I'm going with you."

"Then he may not trust me."

"Too bad. Tell him you didn't feel comfortable coming alone, and that he can trust me. You'll be there. You'll have money. He won't back down."

"You sound so sure. What do you know about buying drugs?"

"Just about as much as you do. I hate raves."

"So do I."

They strolled along through SoHo in no hurry to get anywhere. The air was that pungent combination of humidity, fog, and pollution that Manhattan can conjure up in the late summer and early fall. For a change Alexa didn't have ten homework assignments, and Sadi was always caught up or ahead of her work. They paused at the corner of Prince and Greene to look at the building with the funky mural of the running lady.

"I need a purse." Alexa stopped in front of a store called Back in Time. "Emma has a whole drawer of cute purses. I think she gets a lot of her stuff here. Her last purchase was a pink flowered shawl with a fringe that probably graced some old lady's table for years."

"Emma wears a shawl?" Sadi stopped and looked in the window. "I've always thought she had a great sense of style."

"Not on her shoulders. She ties it around her waist and lets it drape down over a skirt. Looks great on Emma. On me, it would probably look like I dragged off my tablecloth by accident."

"You've got style. Sort of." Sadi jumped back as Alexa took a swing at her. "And that new cap you bought makes you look really sexy. I'm going to get one."

"People will think you're selling newspapers."

Sadi mimed selling papers. "Extra. Extra. Alexa Kane's a spy for the FBI."

Alexa laughed. "Look. There, in the window. That's kind of cute." Alexa pulled open the door to the shop, knowing Sadi would follow her.

The smell of age, dust, musty clothing, heavy perfume, and a huge bouquet of fresh irises filled the air. Sadi sneezed.

"It's okay. I'm allergic to dust."

"Since when?" Alexa knew everything there was to know about Sadi. She'd never been allergic to anything before.

"Since now. Or maybe it's the perfume."

The woman wearing the perfume walked toward them. She was tall with a mop of red hair. Skillfully dyed or real? Her dress was vintage thirties, hitting her mid-calf. But she was thin enough so that it looked rather stylish, especially with a pair of four-inch Manolos, which Alexa could never have walked across the room wearing.

"Cute shoes," Sadi said, probably thinking the same thing.

"End of summer sale. I could never afford them otherwise. But every woman needs at least one pair of Manolos. Don't you think?"

"Sure. I love them." Sadi turned away, pretending to look into another glass-fronted case at jewelry.

"What are you looking for?" the woman asked. "Anything in particular?"

"I think my sister gets all her cute purses here," Alexa said. "That one in the window is cute. I think it's mesh---with the fringe on the bottom." Alexa pointed to the purse.

"Oh, yes, that one is special. But it may be a bit pricy for your budget." The clerk reached for it, handed it to Alexa. "Two hundred dollars."

"Oh." Alexa looked at the purse. It was heavier than she'd expected, not to mention more expensive. "Maybe one more practical, then, one I can carry all the time."

Alexa had no intention of carrying a purse all the time, but the woman would understand what she was saying. Cheaper.

"Look at these here in the back." The woman had to take small steps because the skirt was tight and the heels tall. Be hard to outrun a criminal dressed like that. But then, she probably didn't chase or run away from criminals unless she had a lot of shoplifters who took two-hundred-dollar purses.

A small table in the back held the kind of thing Alexa wanted. She had several choices. Picking up one made of dark red velvet or velour, some soft material, Alexa peeked inside. Room for a cell, lipstick, pen and notepad, keys, a little money.

"How much for this one?"

"Five dollars," the woman replied, smiling.

Alexa put the strap over her shoulder, then tried it over her left shoulder but at her waist on the right so the purse would stay with her if she was running. Who did she plan to run from? Peter? Billy

Razzi? Her mind was going off in all directions now. She shook her head, pulled out the credit card she rarely used, and paid for the purse.

"I'll wear it." She signed the receipt, and waved at Sadi, who was trying on a big hat with an ostrich plume off one side.

"Enjoy it and come back any time," the shop keeper said, giving them a little finger wave.

"You didn't want the two-hundred-dollar purse?" Sadi asked once they were outside.

"Too small." Alexa grinned and skipped down the sidewalk.

"Yeah, I agree." Sadi played along.

"I have an idea." Alexa stopped. "Know how we always joke about visiting the SoHo psychic? Today is the perfect day to check her out."

"I don't believe in that crap." Sadi looked at the storefront that announced tarot readings, palm reading, past and future revealed. "If you were a real psychic, would you have to advertise your ability? Would you have a store where people could come in? That's like a booth at a carnival."

"Why not? How else do you get customers? List in the Yellow Pages?"

"Word of mouth. Or you could concentrate and will people to find you and ask for help."

Alexa shook her head and smiled. "I'll pay. Dad gave me an allowance from the cops in case I needed money. Like tonight. I'll need money to get some pot, and I'm not spending my practically non-existent savings."

"Do you have to turn in an expense report? Won't someone question visiting a psychic as a legitimate expense?"

"Maybe." Alexa laughed.

A bell tinkled when the door opened. The store had dim light. There were all sorts of things to buy. Candles, tarot cards, incense, bottles, and potions. Strange oils and a selection of teas were contained in jars. Crystals of all sizes hung from cords. Madame Maria sat behind a counter reading a newspaper. Alexa felt a little disappointed that she wasn't dressed in a long skirt, a colorful head wrap, her fingers covered with rings. Alexa pretended there was someone else in the back.

"Is the psychic here?" she asked.

"I'm Maria Borgeois. Did you girls want your fortunes told? Cards read? Past life regression? You haven't been in this life long enough to make it interesting. But you might have a really fascinating past life or two."

Alexa felt Sadi's knee on her behind. She wobbled, catching herself on the counter. "Sorry, sometimes I'm a klutz. Has to do with a growth spurt." She was making a terrible fool of herself. "I think we'd like tarot readings. How much—"

"Twenty-five dollars for a half hour. But sometimes I get interested and run over. I'm not very busy today."

"When are you busy?" Sadi asked.

"Weekends, summertime, holidays. Course, I have my regular customers. Some of them call me."

"You can do readings on the phone?" Alexa blurted out.

"Sure. Especially once I get to know someone." Madame Maria got up and motioned for the girls to follow her behind the counter and into a curtained-off back room.

The lighting was dim here too, almost dark. There was the smell of incense in the air, a sweet, rather cloying floral scent. A table was covered by a colorful shawl with a fringe around the bottom. One chair sat behind the table, two in front of it.

"I thought you'd have a crystal ball," Sadi said.

"You know, girls, if you're here for a lark, that's okay. But if you think I'm a phony, that doesn't set well with me. Not all psychics use a crystal ball. I happen to prefer tarot cards. I also read jewelry and other metals, and I can read off an article of clothing or a personal item, like a comb."

Suddenly Maria's voice had become low, serious, professional. She motioned for Alexa and Sadi to sit down.

"To be frank, Maria, I don't know if I believe in this or not," Alexa said. "I guess we did stop on a whim, but I need some help gathering information, and if you see anything while you're reading the cards that you think might help me, I'd be grateful."

"Okay, let's see what we get. Before I use the cards, give me something personal you have that belongs to someone else."

Alexa thought. She didn't... Yes, she did. One thing. She dug the scrap of paper from her pocket with the two names on it. She folded it so Maria couldn't read the names.

Maria took the paper, held it between both hands, closed her eyes, and breathed deeply several times. "The person who wrote this is extremely unhappy. It's hard for me to stand her pain." Maria handed back the paper quickly.

Alexa felt tears rush to her eyes. She looked down and blinked. When she looked up again, Maria was spreading out a deck of tarot cards in front of her on the table scarf. She turned the cards over, one at a time, looking at it, studying it carefully. As she worked, she seemed to be reluctant to turn over each card.

"You're unhappy, too, but you're handling it better, Alexa. Did you recently lose someone close to you? I'm thinking it was your mother. For a woman to lose her mother is devastating, even if you weren't close. And now you're the oldest woman in your family. But women don't come into their own until they lose their mothers. You will find yourself growing more powerful as time passes. The grief will always be there, but you can use it and learn from the pain."

Sadi took Alexa's arm. "Al, are you all right?"

Alexa couldn't even speak. She nodded, holding back all the sorrow, grief, tears she had tried to lock up inside and not give in to. She had cried, of course, but then had tried to be tough.

"Should I go on?" Maria paused, the deck of cards in one hand, a single card in the other.

"Yes," Alexa managed. "I'll be all right. I–I didn't expect you to–to–"

"I'm just telling you what I see. Go home and cry, Alexa. Cry and cry and cry until you can't cry anymore. There's no shame in that. Healing can start from there."

Maria added cards to the spread. Alexa breathed deeply and got control of her emotions, then watched as Maria dealt the pieces of colorful cardboard and laid them in a pattern. She moved slower and slower, frowning, studying the cards.

Since Alexa had never had this done before, she didn't know what to expect, but even she could see that all the cards that Maria was laying out pictured swords. The bottom was a whole row of swords, two, three, five, seven, eight, nine, ten, and page. Then there were the Tower and Emperor cards, The nine of swords was particularly disturbing. A woman sat crying, it seemed, swords covering the wall behind her. The three of swords pictured a large red heart pierced with three swords. Alexa shivered as she studied the eight. The woman was tied up and blindfolded and–

"You know, Alexa, I think this reading is over." Maria's voice and her face reflected fear. Quickly she gathered the cards, took a deep breath, different from the meditative breaths she'd taken earlier. "I can't take this reading further. And I'm not going to charge you."

"Why? I mean, why can't you go on?" A wave of fear replaced the deep sorrow that Alexa had let come to the surface. "What did you see? Was it something bad, scary?"

"I'm just going to tell you to be careful in the next few days."

"Isn't there a card that means death?" Sadi finally spoke. "Did you see that one?"

"Each card has several meanings, Sadi. The card you're thinking of might mean the end of a relationship, breaking up with a boy friend, giving up a friendship. It might mean you can finally bury something from the past. I have never seen someone's death come up in the cards. I don't see it now. That's not why I stopped."

"But you saw something you didn't want to tell me," Alexa said. "Tell me. I'm strong. I need to know."

"I don't know what it means. Just listen to me and be careful. Now, I'd like you to leave. I'm closing up." She tucked the twenty and the five dollar bill into Alexa's hand and closed her fist over it. "Don't argue with me. Just leave."

In seconds Alexa and Sadi found themselves out on the sidewalk in front of the big window with its colorful signs.

"Wow, Al, I think we got more than we bargained for. I wish we hadn't gone in there." Sadi put her arm around Alexa and hugged her.

"Don't let her scare you. I think that was all an act. A good one, but an act just the same."

Alexa pulled out a tissue and blew her nose. She didn't know what to think.

"I need some food," Sadi said. "Let's go see what your dad has for dinner. But don't tell him what we just now did, Al. He'll laugh at us."

"Yeah. He will. We'll laugh at ourselves tomorrow."

I *hope*, Alexa added to herself. What had the psychic seen? She knew Maria had seen something that frightened her. Was it about Alexa or Sadi? Or someone else? Emma? Her father? Not knowing made Alexa even more apprehensive. If there was danger ahead, Alexa wanted to know what it was so she could be ready.

Chapter 10

Alexa's father was taking a dish of manicotti from the oven when they came into the loft. He took a round loaf of anise-flavored bread from the other small warming oven and sliced it. Then he brought a bowl of tossed salad greens over to the table.

"Good timing, don't you think?" Her father moved over to the table to sip a glass of wine he'd been drinking as he cooked. He studied both girls as if he knew something strange or upsetting had happened to them. His intuition had been honed as a cop on the street, and it hadn't gone away with his change in careers.

Alexa and Sadi each hurried to the kitchen and loaded a plate with the spicy manicotti, buttered a slice of bread, and sat at the table with him. Sadi jumped back up to serve Mr. Kane's plate. Alexa wasn't sure she could eat, but the food smelled so good, she was going to try. She took deep breaths and tried to put the psychic and her strange behavior out of her mind.

"I think we'd lose weight if you didn't cook, Tony," Sadi said. "Chinese food has no calories at all."

"Glad I can be of service. Anything exciting happen at school today?" Alexa's father poured himself another glass of the dark red burgundy.

"Nothing exciting," Alexa said. "I'm looking forward to college. Something challenging besides math." She didn't look at Sadi, knew Sadi wouldn't tell what they'd really been doing.

Alexa and Sadi cleaned their plates without talking about anything serious, gathered up the dishes, rinsed them, and quickly placed them in the dishwasher.

"We have to study, Dad. Thanks for dinner." Alexa gave her father a quick hug and kiss on the cheek.

He studied both girls carefully. Alexa knew he sensed there was something they weren't telling him. "Any time. How can I go wrong feeding two beautiful women?"

Sadi closed Alexa's door behind them. "Your dad knew there were things we weren't telling him. I hope I won't get indigestion from eating so fast." She sat down behind Alexa's computer.

"Yeah, it's tough living with a detective. You going to Google?" Alexa took out the scrap of paper where she had listed the spread that had spooked Maria the psychic.

Sadi looked at it as the computer booted up. "There was no six of swords. Or four. I think this one was a five." Sadi pointed to the four that Alexa had scribbled.

"Okay, here it is. Sadi pulled up tarot cards, and their meanings. "Of course, the combination is important," she said, scrolling down to swords. "Let's see the layout again."

"Two, three, five, seven, eight, nine, ten of swords. The Tower, the Wheel of Fortune. Wasn't there a Page? And the Emperor."

Sadi kept jumping around before Alexa could study what was on the screen. "Emperor, I want to know what that means. A powerful, possibly dangerous male figure of authority. Hmmm."

"Could he be young?" Alexa wondered, since the information just said male.

"Why not? But do teenaged boys have a lot of power?"

"They think they do." Alexa smiled, remembering all the guys who had hit on her recently. She glanced at her watch, suddenly remembering she was supposed to meet Billy Razzi at nine o'clock."

"You going somewhere?" Sadi noticed Alexa's obsession with her watch.

"I told Billy Razzi I'd meet him at The Blue Orchid at nine o'clock. Remember?"

"That's right. You think we can sneak out past your father?"

"I shouldn't have to sneak if I'm working for him. I'll just tell him I'm following up a lead. I tried to buy some drugs from Billy in the hall. When I gave that scrap of paper to Madame Maria, I thought she might tell me about the names written on it. Instead she picked up on Emma's feelings. But I'll confirm that he's dealing at the club tonight."

"What are you going to get?"

"Just pot. Even with the money Dad gave me for what he called research, I doubt I have enough to buy anything else. All I want to do is know that Billy is selling. I might get some idea while I'm there of who is supplying him."

"Probably that Emperor guy." Sadi looked back at the screen. "A two of swords suggests danger but that it's within your control."

"Thank goodness. Look, an eight and a nine suggest being afraid and unaware of the exact danger. I think any time you're dealing with people who sell drugs, there's a certain amount of danger, don't you?"

"You can't investigate a crime or criminals without some danger."

Sadi turned to Alexa. "Al, why are you doing this? It's not too late to back out. Go to FBI school or whatever, learn to be a policewoman or agent before you go off free-lancing. You're making me nervous."

"If there are two of us–"

"We could both get killed." Sadi grimaced and turned back to the computer.

They studied the cards for a few minutes longer, then gave it up. Reading tarot cards wasn't something you learned in a few minutes, either, but it might be a safer task to take on.

"If we're going out at nine, I think I'd better tell my parents I'm spending the night here." Sadi pulled out her cell and dialed home. No one was there, so she left a message. "Mom, Dad, it's Sadi. I'm at Alexa's and we're studying for a test. I think I'd better stay here tonight. Love you. See you tomorrow."

Her mom and dad wouldn't be surprised. Sadi spent the night at Alexa's so often, she had the bottom drawer of a chest of drawers for emergency changes of clothes.

"Okay, one hour of studying if we can take a cab there," Sadi declared, her discipline kicking in.

"Yeah, the research slush fund, remember?" Alexa flopped on her futon while Sadi stayed at the desk. Al did a couple of stretches, then opened her chemistry book. She stared at it, but the words and figures all ran together.

Sadi was right, she didn't know what she was doing with this investigation. Why in the world had her father told the police she could do this? Sure, she had a fair amount of self confidence, and she knew self defense, but that didn't make her Super Woman.

Her father had this bad habit of thinking she could do anything, and his attitude had gotten stronger since her mother died. He had fought hard to be independent, yet he leaned on Alexa for a lot of things, mostly emotional support and Emma-sitting.

But ever since her mother had died, Alexa had felt an ache inside her that had nothing to do with loss. It had everything to do with feeling restless. The police station where her father worked had a counselor on staff. Their father had made her and Emma go see the woman, and he had kept on going for sometime. Alexa suspected that Emma just sat quietly while Dr. Headly had talked and encouraged her to talk.

Alexa had listened to the words that Dr. Headly said about loss and grief and the stages of grief—all the things you can read in a good self-help book. How could Alexa tell this woman that she'd been feeling strange even before her mother died? Days were full of school and homework, Tae Kwon Do classes, meets, and talking with Sadi. Maybe it was the routine that was getting old.

Alexa's nights were often filled with wild and crazy dreams, dreams that woke her up sweating and tossing about until Black Bart moved to a chair to sleep. Dreams that had no explanation.

The dreams had tapered off until Lexie died. This last two weeks had been restless and troubled. She had sensed a strength and empathy from the psychic she hadn't felt from the counselor. She wondered if she went back alone, the woman would try again to read her cards or even just talk to her?

A tiny beep made her jump. She looked at Sadi who swung her chair around and closed her book. "Time to go, unless you've changed your mind."

"Nope. The Blue Orchid is a place to dance, isn't it? I guess we should dress the part."

"We have five minutes to get ready. Add a scarf or something and change pants. Cargo pants aren't exactly glamorous." Sadi laughed.

Sadi dug a pair of blue capri pants from her drawer, tied a scarf around her neck. Slipped out her studs and put on a pair of dangly earrings. Kicked off her clogs and slipped into black flats designed to match anything.

Alexa was equally adept at changing clothes. She slipped into the outfit she'd worn to the party with Peter and grabbed the new small purse that she'd bought at the antique shop. She liked the soft material that was her favorite color and the long chain that she could throw over her shoulder to keep her hands free.

Cabs circled through SoHo on a regular basis. The girls had only to raise their hands to make one screech to a halt. Sure enough, the driver was Ralph. This did not seem like a coincidence. He had taken looking after her to a higher level. Had her father or John Blackwood told Ralph about TIF? Had Ralph been working undercover all these years since he had to leave the police?

"Do you have a cell phone, Ralph?" Alexa asked.

"Sure, want to use it?"

"Did my father call you?"

"Why would he do that?"

Alexa shrugged. "The Blue Orchid." She tried to ignore Ralph looking them over in the rearview mirror. She smeared her mouth with the lipstick she'd tossed in the purse. Blackwell was right. She did like pink.

Ralph hadn't driven for long when Alexa realized she had no idea where they were, except that they were driving west. They passed shops with metal doors or gates and windows that could be closed and locked at night. Garages and gas stations. An abandoned movie theater rose up on a corner, a relic of the forties or fifties. Then grimy, dirty warehouses loomed, dark and shabby looking, surely abandoned. Occasionally one had burned, leaving a black skeleton of charred wood and steel.

Light was dim or nearly non-existent where street lamps had burned out or been shot out, or someone was very accurate with rock throwing. Very few people were on the street and those that were walked fast, hurrying, without looking right or left. They seemed eager to reach some destination, God knows where.

"Do people live down here, Ralph?" Alexa asked.

"Not if they can help it."

"Where are we? Are you sure you know where you're going?"

"I know every street in New York, Miss Kane." Ralph sounded offended. "This is the Port Authority area, probably the last area of New York left that needs to be cleaned up. Rent is cheap. That's why nightclubs have sprung up down here. You don't want to be out walking. Once you get inside this place, you stay inside until you get a ride home, you hear?"

"Okay, Ralph." Alexa smiled at Ralph's father-like lecture. "I'll call a cab from inside and wait inside until it comes."

Alexa and Sadi slid out and tossed Ralph his money, ignoring the question on his face. He really wanted to know why they'd come here. Did she need another father looking after her? She stood outside the building, obviously a converted warehouse. Darkness surrounded them. If there had been streetlights here, someone had smashed them all. The music reached out of the club and enticed them to enter.

Alexa looked at Sadi, who shrugged. "We sure don't want to stand out here long. This ain't your grandmother's Tupperware party."

Alexa smiled and took a deep breath. When she had to do something that frightened her, she had taught herself to enter the fear, make it part of her, walk through it. However, fear up till now had been a test at school or getting a new color belt in her karate class.

It took all her willpower to move to the head of the line that waited outside, smile and slip the doorkeeper her new ID card, and a twenty dollar bill, hoping that was enough. When the doorman looked her over, smiled back, and waved her and Sadi in, despite protest from the head of the line, they hurried inside the club.

Alexa felt a wave of relief. *Research*, she reminded herself. *This is just research*. Nightclub hopping was out of her range of experience, was out of her comfort range, but she had a feeling tonight was important. She was sure she'd get information she needed to push this case forward.

Chapter 11

The music was so loud, they couldn't have communicated if they'd have wanted to. Alexa took Sadi's hand and pulled her through the crowd to the bar. Billy had said he'd meet her there. She looked around, but didn't see him or anyone else she knew. Guys oogled both of them, grinned, and started to approach them, but Alexa turned her back. Sadi did the same, put her arm around Alexa's shoulders, and leaned in close to Alexa, as if they were more than friends. That should discourage the guys.

"Nice place, Al. Order me something stronger than orange juice, and laugh as if I just said something really funny."

Sadi's comment relaxed Alexa a little. She laughed and felt some fear fall away. "Two Cokes," she told the bartender, who gave her the once over, probably glad they didn't order alcohol. As if he'd check an ID. But, maybe he would. Alexa wasn't exactly experienced with this scene.

"Maybe we should have invited Peter to come with us," Alexa whispered.

"And admit we were nervous to come here alone?" Sadi smiled

and took the Coke. "That we were mere girls who couldn't take care of ourselves."

"Yes."

Alexa took a big pull on the straw in her drink and let the caffeine and sugar raise her energy level. She did a little bit of huffy breathing to create energy, too.

"Come here often?" A low voice beside Alexa cut through the pounding music that matched the beat of her heart.

She turned and Billy Razzi grinned at her, his green eyes laughing as if he knew they were uncomfortable. "You look a little out of place, but I'll bet we could fix that. A dash of rum in your Coke, maybe some nose candy, if you can afford it. I sometimes give out samples." He grinned again and leaned in way to close to Alexa. He had no appeal to her whatsoever, but she reminded herself that she was not here to flirt.

"We're fine." Alexa looked back at the writhing dancers.

"Dance with me."

"What?"

"This is a place to dance. I'm asking you to dance with me. I like to get to know someone better before I take them into my confidence."

Alexa looked at Sadi. "Will you be all right?"

Sadi's eyes flashed to black, her fighting eyes. "What do you think?"

"Keep me in sight and don't go off alone." Alexa felt like a fool giving Sadi such instructions. Her nerves had turned her into a blithering idiot.

She left her Coke on the bar and moved into the sweaty mass with Billy. Moving to the beat was easy. It didn't take long to let the music move through her and almost relax.

"I knew you wanted to dance. All work and no play—"

"This is not exactly work." Alexa grinned at him. Might as well have some fun and pretend she did this every night. Had he used the word work by accident, or did he suspect she was snooping around for someone?

She used all her wiles to make him forget, if he suspected, that she was a snoop. Letting the music take over her body, she danced as if she knew how. Maybe she had her father's or mother's dancing genes. Both of them loved to go. Not to a place like this, of course. More to places where married adults hung out, and where police and firemen hung out. They liked folk dancing. Her mother told her once about a restaurant that had great Bulgarian food and a wild dance party on Thursday nights.

"You've got good moves. You should come here again." Billy looked down at her and smiled. "With me."

She didn't answer. No way was she going to date Billy Razzi.

When they returned to the bar where Sadi waited, having fended for herself fine, it seemed, Alexa reached for her Coke.

"Don't drink that." Billy knocked her hand away and pushed the drink to the back of the slick wood. "Rufies are cheap."

Date rape drugs. The first thing girls learned in Drugs 101. What was Alexa thinking? She wasn't. Engage brain. She smiled at Billy. "Thanks. We can't stay long."

"Okay." Billy tipped his head toward a dark corner. "What is it you want?"

"Just pot. I told you." She moved away from the bar and into the shadows with him.

"Baby steps?" Even in the dim light she could see his white teeth and expensive smile. Someone cared enough to put him in braces. "Okay, twenty will get you a starter supply. He motioned her to follow him farther into the dark hallway, took her purse, placed a small packet inside, studied the contents, and pulled out a twenty dollar bill. "Come back when you graduate from this." He smiled again. "Or if you just want to dance."

He handed her the closed purse and then slipped into the shifting shadows that surrounded the flashing colored lights on the dance floor. She couldn't have followed him if she'd wanted to.

Let him go. She really was satisfied with baby steps. She had confirmed that Billy Razzi was another source for drugs at the high school. Emma's note and Alexa's being here tonight had done that much for her.

"Now can we go home?" Sadi said, when Alexa fought her way back to the bar.

"My idea exactly." She dug into her purse for her cell and dialed the cab company's number.

Alexa had the cab—not Ralph this time, which made her feel better—drop Sadi off at her place, then take her home. She appreciated his waiting until she waved and slipped inside her building.

Her dad was waiting up for her. "Moonlighting?" he asked with a smile, not scolding her, but curious.

"Dancing," Alexa said, grabbing a tall glass of ice water and flopping on the couch beside her dad's wheelchair. "No one told me that undercover work could be fun." She didn't mention the fear before she'd left home and gotten into the bar tonight.

"You find a trail and follow it down, just like an old bloodhound, his nose on the scent. No howling," he teased.

"Dad, I got one piece of information. Billy Razzi is also selling at the high school. He pretended he didn't have anything at school and made me go to this nightclub, but he sold me some marijuana. Not much, but he mentioned other things he could get."

"Okay, I'll pass that information on. We won't arrest him yet. I think since the cops had leads, they should have followed them up, not bring in Griffin and Platt. We had no leads the minute we pulled them in. They weren't going to talk, and usually a supplier knows only the guy above him, the one who supplies him. They don't know who the big boys are."

The Emperor, Alexa thought. "The pawn doesn't know the king?"

"Right. Want to play a game?"

Alexa often played chess with her father, but did he realize how late it was on a school night?

"Beauty sleep, remember, Dad? Rain check for the weekend."

Beauty sleep would have been nice. No sooner had Alexa undressed, washed her face, and brushed her teeth, slipped into her soft cotton nightshirt, did she fall asleep. And for a short while she was so tired she slept deeply. Then the dreams started:

She was in a small, confined place. All around her stood shadowy men, people, holding swords.

Two swords to the front. As she turned, four swords on her right, six at her back, three on her left. She put out both hands and the swords moved back just enough so she couldn't touch them. Gray, pewter, wide, heavy blades, dull with enough polish to flicker and flash when an unknown source of light let her see them. The blades formed a fence that kept her inside, trapped. They didn't threaten in any way except to be there, rowed up like a picket fence that had never been white.

She remembered her skills and kicked out, expecting to hear the clank and crash as she knocked blades to the floor. No sound. Complete silence. But the swords did part and reconfigure to form a door.

Should she step through? She was trapped but at the same time safely confined. The swords did not threaten. Could they be protecting her? She hesitated, but didn't like the feeling of being inside the circle.

She moved forward one step, two, three. The swords moved back just enough, not leaving, but giving way.

Then she heard the weeping. She stepped into the room.

A woman sat on a bed, her head in her hands. On the wall behind her hung swords. Alexa counted. Nine swords, the nine of swords. A woman in distress.

"Please, please help me," the woman pleaded without looking up. "My dreams, a nightmare, I'm in danger. Please help me."

Alexa stepped back. The wall of swords closed up again, surrounding her, trapping her, keeping her confined. She pushed against the cold, flat steel blades. The metal was unyielding. She spun around, looking for another way out. No way out. She was again trapped.

"I can't help you, I'm sorry, I can't. I can't help myself."

Alexa had spoken the words aloud, waking herself up. Black Bart was a dark shadow sitting beside her. She knew he was looking at her, disgusted that she had moved so abruptly.

She pulled the big, warm cat into her arms, and for a few seconds he allowed her to hold him.

"I can't help her, Bart. I can't help myself."

Bart squirmed away, and Alexa, feeling bereft and helpless, cried herself back to sleep.

Chapter 12

By morning, Alexa had gotten over the midnight shadows of her dreams, but she felt exhausted and discouraged. What made her think she could be an undercover police teen? What made her father or the suits think she could?

However, something kept niggling at the back of her brain.

She sleep-walked through breakfast and the trip to school. Sadi, lost in her own thoughts, as she often was, stayed quiet. Without a word, they crossed the street so they didn't have to walk past the window of the SoHo psychic. By then, though, Alexa suspected that if she looked at Sadi, both would burst out giggling. Her mood was lifting.

By third period English class, Alexa felt as if she was going to burst with something, and she didn't even know what. It wasn't energy. She wished she had eaten more breakfast.

The assignment was an essay on teen responsibility. Mrs. Kleisters had talked for a few minutes, helping the students kick-start their thinking, but Alexa had heard very little she said. Something about how much responsibility did they have, how much did they want?

Could they handle more than they had now?

Not much. In fact right now, Alexa wished she didn't have any. She wished she had only herself to look after and worry about, and would she make a mess of that?

Pulling a sheet of paper from her notebook, she tried a method of brainstorming she'd learned way back in grade school for pulling out whatever was nagging at her subconscious.

In the center of the page, inside a balloon, she wrote the word "Emperor." The idea had come from the tarot cards, of course, so maybe the visit to Maria wasn't totally a waste of time. All around the center balloon, she filled other circles with words.

Emperor, king, China, Chinese food, noodles. She hesitated. Nothing was too silly or crazy to put down. She was brainstorming, thinking, going into her right brain, the side that was supposed to be creative. Don't let me down now, she thought, and that pulled her out of her stream of consciousness. Doing this while she was hungry might be a mistake.

Emperor, restaurants, names of restaurants, The Blue Orchid, not a restaurant, a nightclub, doesn't matter, convenient market, black market, pipeline for drugs. Comes in with food and drinks, labeled as food, easy to disguise anything illegal.

"Looking for an idea, Miss Kane?" a voice above her said, a teacher voice. Ms. Kleisters looked at her paper and frowned.

"Yes, I'm almost there." Alexa hid her paper as much as she dared. What did Chinese nightclubs have to do this? And who said The Blue Orchid had anything to do with Chinese food or drink? She never saw anyone in there who looked Asian. There was no connection, but the pipeline idea might be key.

Maybe the head of the drug ring that the police wanted her to find owned The Blue Orchid, which gave him a cover for smuggling drugs or anything he liked into Manhattan. New York was a port. Dozens of ships came in every day. Were they all inspected?

Okay, food and drink came to the nightclub from all over the country, maybe. Maybe she was out on a limb here. It didn't matter who supplied the club with anything. What mattered was who was in charge. And just the fact that Billy Razzi asked her to meet him there, since he was supposedly out of drugs, and that when she did meet him there, he had what she wanted. And more, she thought, since he hinted of having anything else she wanted.

There. She was onto something. She was sure.

The buzzer rang for the period to be over. She hadn't written a word. "Finish this tonight for homework," Kleisters said. "Due tomorrow. Some of you can read to us, put us to sleep before lunch."

She looked at Alexa when she said that, but maybe her gaze was coincidence. She had to look at someone.

Alexa could certainly write about the responsibility that had fallen on her shoulders, but, of course, she wouldn't. Unless she wrote in general about teens being able to do much more than adults gave them credit for.

"Get your essay written, Al?" Peter Talbott stopped at her desk before she could stand up. "Looks like a lot of scribbling to me."

Alexa folded her paper immediately and stuck it in her pocket. "Scribbling is often a good way to get an idea." She smiled at Peter.

He followed her out of the room. "Going to lunch? Want to leave campus and go eat someplace else?"

"Not enough time. Besides there are lots of choices here. And I'm too hungry to go far."

She got in the line for the grill. "Hamburger, fries, chocolate milkshake," she told one of the cooks. She didn't even have to make a decision. Her stomach growled.

Peter smiled when he heard her order. "Takes a lot of food to keep a hottie like you up and running."

"Hotties burn up a lot of calories. Don't you know that?"

He didn't fall into the trap of answering her, just said, "The same," to the woman behind the counter.

"I can match you calorie for calorie. We could go dancing after school if we have energy left."

"Dancing after school? You have to be kidding."

"I think that place you were in the other night opens at five o'clock. Probably not much action until later, though. My sister went there after school. They let people who might not be eighteen in for early-hour dancing."

"Did Emma go there, too?" Alexa felt sick to her stomach. The French fry heading for her mouth stopped in mid-air.

"I'm sure all the fearless foursome did. Lots of ninth graders can pass for eighteen, but like I say, the doorman turns his head until about eight o'clock."

"You seem to know all the ins and outs of this place. How often do you go?" And how did Peter know she was at The Blue Orchid? Was he there? In such a crowd, she could have missed him. Or had he followed her there? She didn't like that idea.

Peter's face turned a very light shade of pink, but it was noticeable in the harsh light of the cafeteria.

"I don't like being home alone all the time. Have to go somewhere. Besides, I like to dance."

"So do I, Peter. But I *have* to study tonight. Some other night—soon."

"Okay, any night you like. Here's my cell number if you change your mind about tonight."

"Why don't you come to the studio and take Tae Kwon Do?"

"I'm too old for that now. I should have started when I was eight, don't you think?"

"I think you can start at any time. You could be in my adult beginners' class."

"You'd be my teacher?" Peter grinned.

"Sure. Why not?"

"Let's stick to dancing.

When Alexa got home from school, she found a note from her father that said he would be out all evening. He'd left money to order pizza. Emma came in right after Alexa.

"Want pizza?" Alexa waved the twenty dollar bill as she picked up the phone. "Dad won't be home."

"Sure. No peppers or anchovies. Anything else is okay."

They could have gone out someplace in the neighborhood, but Alexa figured she could do her English essay while she ate. She got it started on the dining table as she waited for the delivery.

Emma was working some math problems, but she grabbed the twenty and answered the door when they heard the buzzer. She placed the box in the middle of the table, and they opened it to take in the heavenly smell of tomato sauce, pepperoni, sausage, and olives.

"Want a beer?" Emma grinned at Alexa.

"Do we need to keep studying?" Alexa grinned back and brought two glasses of unsweetened iced tea, a stack of napkins, and two plates to the table. She hadn't had nearly enough sleep this week. A beer would knock her right out.

Both ate and concentrated on homework for a few minutes. Alexa reached for another slice of the pizza, looked at Emma's mop of blonde hair, and decided to risk questioning her.

"Emma, Peter said the four of you often went to The Blue Orchid after school."

"So. It's a good place to dance." Emma didn't look at Alexa, just kept working and eating. The question had brought on Emma's prickly defense system, but Alexa kept talking.

"How'd you get in? Isn't there an age thing?"

Emma shrugged. "Lexie knew the guy at the door, and he knew she always had a twenty in her pocket. They don't care."

"They could lose their liquor license."

"We drank Cokes. He made that clear to us when he let us in the first time."

"This could be important, Emma. Did you ever see anyone buying drugs while you were there?"

"Not really. But everyone knows you can get stuff there."

"Is that where you got the Ecstasy?"

Emma bit her lip. "No. Bernadette said she'd bring us what we wanted to school. She wasn't supposed to let us have it at the nightclub. I guess it's like the liquor license."

Yeah, Alexa thought. *They could lose their license to sell drugs.* If pot ever became legal, she guessed places would have pot licenses just like liquor licenses. And legal ages to smoke.

"Did you ever see anyone older there, someone who looked like he might own the place?" Alexa kept picking at Emma's brain, thinking Emma might know something she'd forgotten, or have seen something she ignored at the time.

"I never paid any attention to the old guys. I guess some were there, but they weren't dancing. I was only interested in someone who wanted to dance. But we danced with each other, too. Why do you want to know? Go over there and check it out. You could get in easy."

"Have you been back since, since–"

"No, I don't much feel like dancing. Are you going to tell me I can't go there any more?"

"I didn't say that. But I'd strongly suggest you don't."

"I'll go wherever I like. Leave me alone. You aren't my mother."

Emma grabbed another slice of pizza, placed it on a napkin, grabbed her book and papers, and fled to her room.

No, I'm not your mother, Emma. I sure wish she was here to help me with you. Alexa was almost sorry she'd questioned Emma. She didn't learn anything new.

She sighed. Her essay was boring. The pizza had settled into a hard lump in her stomach. She toyed with the idea of calling Peter and saying she'd go out after all.

No, if she was with Peter, she'd dance, she'd enjoy it, but she wouldn't learn anything. She'd go back to The Blue Orchid alone.

Chapter 13

Alexa dressed carefully again, remembered what John Blackwood said about looking sexy, dressing older. She was careful, though, not to overdo the sexy part, since she was going alone.

She glanced in the mirror of her dresser, and liked what she saw. Reaching for a lipstick, she saw the one John Blackwood had given her, the James-Bond-toy lipstick. The color matched her outfit. A mirror ran down the side. But more importantly the base contained the tracking device. She turned the bottom one time to turn run the lipstick up. Then carefully, she turned the second ring to turn on the device. Someone, she hoped, at the station, or someplace, would now track where she went. She had called Blackwood twice before tonight to tell him she was going to The Blue Orchid and the little bits of information she'd picked up.

Alexa didn't call for a cab, but flagged one on the street. She didn't want Ralph frowning at her for going out alone.

Without saying a word, the cabbie drove the same seedy route that was both frightening and depressing to Alexa. Her father had told her how Mayor Rudy Giuliani had cleaned up the theater district so people felt safe going there. Why couldn't the new mayor do something to clean up this neighborhood?

The cab driver looked her over as she dug in her purse for money, but it wasn't a looking-after-her look. He was younger and less nosy. He did however say, "Have fun," as she paid him. Then he locked his doors and pulled away from the curb without looking back.

Heavy metal spilled out onto the sidewalk. The music filled Alexa, disturbed her with its intrusive beat. They'd have live bands later in the evening, some of them better than whoever made this CD.

Alexa flashed her false ID, tried to look casual, even bored. She didn't offer the doorman any money. He'd seen her before, and she was spending enough money on cabs and buying pot.

She didn't see anyone she knew inside the club. Suddenly, just hanging out here seemed counterproductive. What was it she expected to hear, see, find out? Someone was supposed to walk by and say, I'm the person you're looking for? She bought a Coke, then stood near the bar, watching the dancers. Over the next forty-five minutes, three guys asked her to dance. She was tempted, especially for one who was really cute. She was bored, but she hadn't come here to dance.

After two Cokes, she made her way to the ladies room, which was down a dark hall that smelled of urine, vomit, and stale sweat. Why didn't someone keep the hall clean, or had they tried and lost their battle?

After she used the toilet, she looked in the cloudy bathroom mirror and smeared on some lipstick. There was nothing she could do about the circles under her eyes. *Go home, Al. Get some sleep.* Good idea.

Back in the crush of bodies, here despite it being a school night, she looked at her watch and decided it *was* time to go home. She longed for her dark, quiet room and Black Bart purring as she did her homework.

On one end of the bar sat a basket of hard candies. She reached for one, unwrapped it as she made her way to the door, popped it in her mouth. Cinnamon, yum.

Someone bumped into her before she squeezed through the crowd. It was the really cute guy.

"You can't leave yet. At least, not until you give me one dance. You promised."

"I did?" Alexa felt a little woozy. She didn't remember promising anyone anything. But she raised both arms and stepped into his arms for a quieter, slower dance. He was smooth, easy to follow, a great dancer.

She stumbled and leaned into him, closer than she meant, too close. His body odor mixed with too much aftershave, and his boozy breath made her dizzy.

"Whoa, that's nice, but are you all right? How many fizzy grapefruit drinks did you have?"

"I was drinking Coke, silly. But I think it's too hot in here." She rubbed her forehead and closed her eyes for a second. "I was going home anyway. The fresh air will help. Sorry. The dance was nice. I'll come back."

He took her arm and helped her walk across the crowded dance floor. People, like a school of wiggling fish, bumped her and kept sliding around her, closing off her escape route.

"Please, please let me through." She put our her hands to make a path. "I have to get outside."

"Barfer coming through," some guy said, laughing. "Make a path."

By magic people stepped back and let Alexa through. The damp night air surrounded her. Fog, mist, spitting cold rain chilled her immediately and made her wish she'd brought a jacket.

She looked around. Her dance partner had disappeared. Where was the doorman? The doors to the club were closed as if it was closed, no more room.

What was wrong with her? She felt totally disoriented. Sitting on the curb sounded like exactly what she needed to do, but the sidewalk, the streets were wet. What little light the street lamp gave off made everything look covered with slime. No way was she sitting down. No way was she passing out either. But....

A car pulled up beside her. Someone stepped from the backseat and took her arm. "Need help?" A low voice spoke and before she could say, "no thanks," he had shoved her into the car.

"Hey," she protested. "I'm going home. I was looking for a cab."

She struggled, but her entire body felt as if it were boneless. All of her self-defense skills were useless when she had no strength to even push against the man who got in beside her.

Inside, the car was dark and smelled of cigarette smoke and a sweet spicy cologne or shaving lotion.

The man on the other side of her slipped a scarf around her eyes, tied it behind her head. The sidewalk man bound her hands together in front of her.

"Please, please don't," she managed to say, but her words came out in a whisper.

"She likes that candy, boss,"

The cinnamon candy? What was it? Was that why she felt so weird, had turned to jelly all over?

She reminded herself to breathe, even through the musty-smelling rag around her face. "Let me go. What do you think you're doing?"

All the men in the car laughed. A voice, slightly familiar, from the front seat said, "Stay out of The Orchid, Miss Kane. It's not really your kind of place."

"Yeah, you could get hurt," the man beside her said. His breath was foul, his mouth way too close to her face. She leaned away from him, but there was so little room in the back seat. She was squeezed between the two men.

She thought of the card, the eight of swords. The woman was tied up, blindfolded, trapped inside the fence of swords.

"This is good," the front voice said. "Stop here."

Alexa's heart pounded, making it even harder to breathe. The car stopped. The back door opened. In seconds two men reached in, dragged her out, lifted her, and tossed her on what seemed like boards, outside, wet. They got back in the car, slammed the doors, their laughter trailing out the windows. The car pulled away, exhaust fumes mixing with the cold, wet air.

Chapter 14

Water. The smell of salt, fish, the sound of waves lapping. A cold wind raked her body, and she knew she had to move.

Her hands weren't bound tightly. She lifted them to her mouth and with her teeth tugged at the strip of cloth that tied them.

As soon as she was free, she grabbed the scarf from her face. Even in the darkness, she knew where she was. The docks. A ship loomed over her from the water. Course, there were lots of docks. Was she uptown or downtown? They hadn't driven far. But she hadn't been able to pay attention. Her brain was still fuzzy. Thinking was difficult, even when she concentrated and tried.

Her purse? Did she still have the small purse with her cell? It had slid around to her back, but she did. Before she could place a call, however, a car screeched to a halt, its lights shining on her.

A man jumped from the car, leaving lights on, the engine running. "Alexa, Al, are you all right?"

Alexa tried to stand up. She almost fell. John Blackwood grabbed her arm. "What's the matter? You—you aren't drunk, are you?"

"No, I don't know what's wrong. I have my cell. I was going to call for help. Oh, did—did the tracking device work?"

"Yes. Sorry it took me so long to get here. I was home when I got the call that the station felt something was wrong. They knew you were at The Blue Orchid, but I had told them that was all right. I knew you had been going there. But when they said you were here, on the docks, we all knew there was a problem."

"You didn't think I was fishing?"

"I'm glad to see you haven't lost your sense of humor."

The word was no sooner out of his mouth when another cop car screeched to a halt just yards from where they stood. Well, Blackwood stood. Alexa was having a hard time managing the simple act. She wobbled and grabbed a piling to hold onto.

"I called your place and asked to talk to you, just double checking. Your father had just gotten home. When you weren't there, I knew you had your lipstick, and that you had used it. Thank God. But maybe you shouldn't have gone there alone."

"I was just hanging out. Watching people. Looking for someone, anyone who looked out of place. I was fine until–until–"

"Until what?" Blackwood took Alexa's arm. "Did someone slip you something? What were you drinking?"

"Coke, and I never set it down and left it. I know better than that. This may sound strange, but there was a basket of hard candies on the bar. I ate one and right after, when I was dancing, I started to feel strange. Then in the car, a man said, something like cinnamon was going to be popular. Does that make any sense to you? Was there something in the candy?"

Blackwood let out the breath he was holding. Then took another and another. "Weed candy. It's fairly new. THC. Kind of like the old pot brownies, but less suspicious. Looks like regular hard candy."

"Pot is in the candy?" Alexa asked.

Blackwood nodded. "Some of it is as strong as smoking a bowl of marijuana. Especially if you aren't used to smoking."

"You could carry it in your purse or pocket and no one would know it wasn't candy," Alexa said. "It looks like hard candy."

"Exactly. Maybe the cost will deter a few. Runs five to fifteen dollars for a couple of pieces."

"This was a free sample, or at least I didn't pay for it."

Alexa had paid for it. The pot had rendered her helpless when the car stopped and that man shoved her in. Otherwise she would have kicked and punched and at least made it harder for them. As it was, she was like a baby kitten without even any claws to defend herself.

And now she felt sick to her stomach and had a pounding headache. "Why did they

pick you up, and why did they leave you here?"

Blackwood took Alexa's arm and led her to his police car. He placed her in the passenger seat, then got in, but didn't drive away immediately.

"I don't know, except to warn me. They could have dumped me off the pier."

"If they'd have wanted you dead, Alexa. You took too big a risk tonight. Promise me you won't do that again. We've got plenty of undercover cops for dates if you want to check out some clubs."

"Not just clubs, but The Blue Orchid." Alexa leaned back against the seat of the car and fought to keep her eyes open and her speech from slurring. "Can you find out who owns that club?"

"Sure. But it may be perfectly legitimate. We can only shut them down if we find out the club is actually dealing or we catch them full of minors drinking booze."

"Emma said they went there, but could only buy soft drinks. And the bouncers kicked them out by eight o'clock to make room for older customers. Blackwood, I met Billy Razzi there. He sold me some pot. He suggested he could get anything else I wanted."

"Doesn't mean he gets his supply at The Orchid, but it might add up. Did you know any of the men in the car, the man who grabbed you off the street and shoved you in?"

"No, but one voice sounded familiar. It was dark and they put a scarf over my face, but mainly I was too drugged to pay a lot of attention. I think they just wanted to warn me to stay out of The Orchid. They made a mistake. If they hadn't done this, I would have had only suspicions. Now, I think I must be getting too close to someone or to learning something they don't want me to know."

"I hate to admit it, since you took this risk tonight, but I think you're right. Hundreds of kids go there to dance. Why would one more upset them? We patrol down there. We even have cops in there at times, the ones who look like teenagers. They're just supposed to keep their eyes open."

Alexa wanted to ask if one of the cops was tall with dark curly hair and blue eyes. A great dancer. She'd like to think he was a cop. Then she might consider dancing with him again.

"I plan to go back," Alexa said, her head starting to clear. "But I won't eat or drink anything or leave with a good-looking stranger." She was able to smile now that she was safe and almost home. Her dad was going to be angry, and she didn't blame him.

One more tarot card popped into her mind. The heart with three swords running through it. *Which could mean anything*, she told herself. *Three guys break your heart all at the same time. Or three try to kill you and succeed.*

Chapter 15

Alexa woke late next morning, feeling as if she had a hangover. Not that she knew exactly what a hangover felt like. She'd never had one. She knew her fuzzy brain was a result of the weed candy she'd eaten by accident. Was it an accident? Or had someone set the tempting basket of what seemed like harmless card candies on the end of the bar just as she'd come out of the bathroom, knowing she'd have to walk right past it?

If that was the case, someone had been watching her all evening. Looking for an opportunity to drug her so they could get her in the car. No way could they have nabbed her otherwise. She'd had a model mugger class where in the exam she'd had to fight off two intruders. She had kicked butt, throwing both guys, passing her test with flying colors. Could she have done it when it was real?

When she looked at her watch, she realized she'd slept through the soft beeping alarm. Nine o'clock. Her cell beeped.

"Sadi?"

"Get up, sleepyhead. Tony wouldn't let me wake you. What happened last night?"

"Long story. Messy one. Scary if I'd care to admit it."

"Does Batman go off without Robin? Does Cat Woman travel without Black Bart? That will teach you to leave your valuable, not to mention loyal, sidekick, your faithful companion behind."

"Faithful companion? That sounds like a dog."

"Bow-wow. Got your back. You coming to school?"

"I don't think so. I feel as if a moving van hit me."

"Peter asked where you were. Should I tell him?"

"No, it's none of his business."

"Tony?"

"He's worried, I can tell. But he knows I'm working. Sadi, I must be getting close to someone. Otherwise, why warm me off?"

"I think you're right. Someone at The Orchid is deep in this mess, and you're making them nervous. Could it be Billy Razzi?"

"No, he's just an underling. I'm after someone at the top, The Emperor, and he knows it."

"And that, fearless friend, sounds dangerous. He's making really big bucks, and you're threatening his bank account. Take my money, but don't take my wife. On second thought, take my wife. I like my money too much." Sadi went into an old Jack Benny routine.

Alexa's dad had videotapes of all the old comedians: Red Skeleton, Marks Brothers, Laurel and Hardy, Jack Benny. He had watched them a lot when he was recovering from the bullet that put him in a wheelchair and while he was in rehabilitation, learning how to be a functioning human again. He said laughter was healing. Alexa wished she had something to laugh about right now.

"Still there?" Sadi asked. "I'm late to chem. I'll stop by after school. Be there. Promise?"

"Promise. I'm going back to sleep."

Alexa slept for another couple of hours. When she got up, drank a strong cup of coffee, ate some breakfast, she started to feel restless. Her dad was off someplace. She realized she hadn't spent a lot of time alone recently, and while being alone was okay, today a solitary afternoon wasn't something she wanted to face.

She stepped out on the street and knew immediately where she was going to go. Please be there. She checked her watch. Most of the SoHo stores didn't open until eleven o'clock. Except for The Cyber Café. She could always stop there for another cup of coffee. One cup hadn't quite made her thinking sharp or her eyes clear. In fact, her whole body still felt fuzzy, but not the warm and fuzzy kind of mood. How could people function under the influence of smoking pot all the time? Maybe they didn't.

At the door to the SoHo Psychic, not just unlocked but standing open, she paused, took a deep breath and stepped inside. Her nostrils filled with incense, and she fought sneezing. She took a deep breath and let the sweet scent flow over her and relax her.

"Yes." Maria came from behind the curtain, but stopped short when she recognized Alexa. "Sorry, I'm not open today."

"Your door was open, you'd be open to someone else." Alexa's determination gene kicked in. "Please, I need to ask you some questions. I need to know why you wouldn't read my cards the other day. Was it because it was almost all swords?"

Maria hesitated, took a deep breath, then gave in to Alexa's request. "Okay, come in back."

Alexa looked around again at the velvet curtains, colorful wall hangings, the dim lights. She inhaled the incense again. "This is all for show, isn't it?" She indicated the trappings of the room. "You don't need it."

"Tourists like it." Maria actually smiled. "You're pretty smart, aren't you? How old are you? Eighteen?"

"Seventeen, actually. Tell me when I was born." Now Alexa was giving Maria a bad time.

"Probably November. Scorpios are the most stubborn people, and straightforward. They get right to the point."

Alexa stifled a giggle. She did have a November birthday.

"I won't put out a full spread again, Alexa. I'll draw three cards. That will have to satisfy you."

As Maria spoke, she shuffled the cards, palmed them in her right hand, and slowly laid three face up. Then she seemed to go into a meditative state and study the cards.

One of the cards was The Tower, which had a frightening picture. The top had blown off the structure, flames shot out the windows, and people fell or jumped to get out.

Alexa waited, wanting to speak, reluctant to interrupt the silence and Maria's thoughts.

"You have sustained a great loss. The grief is still with you. Heavy."

Alexa nodded. "My mother died two years ago." She had already told Maria that.

"You are taking a great risk."

Alexa nodded and waited. She had no plan to tell Maria anything about what she was doing, her new job, give her any information. Maria remained silent.

Finally Alexa lost patience. "How will this risk play out? Can you see?"

"No, but if I could, I wouldn't say. I don't know. The result is up to you. You are in charge of the situation. Your choices will determine the ending."

Silence again.   Alexa wanted more answers, some concrete suggestions or facts or help.

"You are a strong woman."

Alexa liked Maria's calling her a woman. She no longer felt like a child.   That was a certainty.   But a woman should have more confidence, more resourcefulness, more verve, wouldn't she? She was caught in some limbo between being a kid and being an adult. A place that was uncomfortable and confusing.

"Something that has been lost will be found."

Now Maria slipped into fortune cookie lines.

"Or changed."

"Changed? How?"

"I can't see that. I don't know. We're finished here." Maria quickly scooped up the three cards and shuffled them back into the deck.

Had Alexa learned anything? Not really, but she felt better. And Maria seemed sincere, not a phony, even if she did work to bring in the tourist trade. Alexa reached for her purse.

"No." Maria's hand raised as if she were pushing Alexa away. "No charge. I frightened you before. I'm sorry. I was also frightened. I felt as if reading your cards would harm both of us. That hasn't happened to me in a long time. If you can fast for the rest of the day, your energy should return. Good luck. Be careful."

Maria pushed through the red velvet curtains across the back of the room and disappeared before Alexa could protest the free reading or say more.

Alexa stopped at the coffee shop instead of fasting. Her idea of help was a double espresso and a sticky bun. She knew that would give her energy for only about half an hour, but the idea of going without eating didn't suit her.

Her cell vibrated. She looked at the number. Blackwood. "Yes, I'm okay, Blackwood. And I know that was stupid. That's one of the things I remember from last night. You going to fuss at me some more?"

"Where are you?"

"At the Cyber Café."

"Stay there. I'm not far away."

Alexa sipped her coffee, ate the sweet roll, and waited. Was she going to get a lecture or some ideas on what to do next?"

Blackwood came into the café in civilian clothes. He looked even younger in jeans and a blue jean shirt, but the short beard and mustache he was growing aged him. And his dark aviator glasses made him look really sexy. Several buttons at the neck of his shirt were unbuttoned, which exposed a leather necklace with a cross on it.

"You Catholic?" she asked after he'd gotten a cup of coffee and sat down.

"My mother raised me in the church. Easy to lose your faith working my job." He grinned.

"Easy to need it, too."

"Yeah, I guess you're right. I found myself praying you were all right last night."

"I'm sorry I took that chance. It didn't seem as if I was taking a chance at the time. I can't help but think there are answers to all our questions at The Blue Orchid, and I guess I thought I'd find them if I hung out there long enough."

"Someone else was afraid you'd find them, too." Blackwood sipped his latte and studied her. "You really have stirred things up. Maybe I should take over from here."

"Listen, you can't have a teen investigator that you pull off the job as soon as things heat up. If I'm going to play with your team, you're going to have to let me stay in the first string."

"Even if you're tackled when you leave yourself unprotected?" Blackwood picked up on the football talk and took it farther. "Did you hear the word, team? That's the idea here. You surround yourself with a few good defenders."

"So I should call you next time I want to go dancing?"

"Please. If I can't go, I'll find someone who can." He put out his hand. "Yes, no matter what time of the day or night you get a wild idea and follow up on it. It's too late to go to school. Can I buy you lunch or walk you home?"

Alexa grinned but shook her head. "Can't eat much yet. And I know the way home. If someone is watching me, we shouldn't be seen together."

"And we have to stop meeting this way?"

"Well, you don't look like that guy in uniform who came to my door a week ago. Taking off the uniform and looking like a teen model is a pretty good disguise."

Blackwood blushed. Alexa laughed, stood, and left him to watch her to the door.

She was back in the loft, deciding how to spend the rest of the day when she got another phone call. This time the real phone in their apartment rang.

"Kane residence."

A voice, electronically altered spoke. "Stay out of this. I can give you only so many warnings before it's too late. Please, Alexa, stop snooping. You underestimate your opponent, the danger."

A click left Alexa holding the receiver, staring at the cradle. A shiver of fear left her terrified and wishing she had taken Blackwood up on his invitation to lunch.

Chapter 16

Fear was not Alexa's style. The shiver that came from the phone call lasted only long enough for anger to kick in. No one was going to keep her frightened in her own home. She had taken a scary job, a job with risks. This wasn't the first, and wouldn't be the last time she'd feel scared. Her dad said one time that if a cop wasn't scared when he went on a call, he didn't want him on his team. Fear sharpened your edges, your sense of alertness, your attention to detail.

She stared at the phone for a few seconds, then grabbed it up and dialed Officer Blackwood's cell, the number he had given her if she needed to reach him in a hurry.

"What's up, Alexa? You change your mind about lunch?" There was a smile in his voice.

"No, thanks. I just wanted you to know that I got a call from some sicko warning me off the case. Can you trace it?"

"Did you recognize the voice? Was it male or female?"

"They used one of those electronic voice scramblers. If I had to say who called, I'll say it was an alien. You know the sound."

"Yeah. Unfortunately, those devices are easy to get hold of and easier to use. But we can track the location of the call. Stay there. If you don't mind, I'll finish <u>my</u> lunch, since I didn't have breakfast. Then I'll get on it and get back to you."

As she hung up the phone and collapsed on a couch, the apartment door opened. Her heart skipped, then she relaxed. Her father wheeled into the room. Was she going to become a scared rabbit, jumping at every sound?

"You didn't go to school when you woke up?" Tony asked. "I left you a note."

She realized she hadn't even checked their small whiteboard in the kitchen. Messages, grocery lists, whatever anyone wanted to say instead of phone between cells.

"Sorry, Dad. I took off as soon as I woke up, but I didn't feel like going to school."

Her father gave her one of his looks, the one that said, anything wrong, want to talk?

"I was still wiped out from the weed. Hard to understand why anyone would pay to feel that way."

"I agree, but half the world seems to want to escape." Her father wheeled himself over to the fridge and grabbed a bottle of water. "Do you have time to go over what you've found out so far? Any leads on who might be head of this drug ring in the high school?"

"No, but I'm making someone nervous." Alexa listed the reasons she thought that. All the warnings, including last night's kidnaping, the phone calls, especially the last one with the altered voice.

"He doesn't want to hurt you, or he would have already."

"You sure? He's making me plenty nervous."

"Don't stop being careful, but violence would probably be his last resort. He's what we call a hand's clean man. He has other people do what he needs done, check in the deliveries, keep an inventory, head up the sales staff. This is a business, Alexa."

Her father pointed the remote control to his CD player, and the mellow jazz piano of Thelonious Monk filled the room. He closed his eyes, but Alexa knew he did that when he was thinking. He said the music helped him think.

Today the music made her feel sad, sad for her father stuck in a wheelchair, sad for herself pretending to be working for the police, solving a crime, but only sitting here wondering what to do next. Okay, confess.

"Dad, I don't know what to do next. Blackwood is trying to trace where the most recent call came from. But that leaves me with no more leads. What would you do?"

Her father looked at her. She couldn't read his expression. "Cook."

"If I cook and eat every time I get stuck with a problem, I'll weigh three hundred pounds." Alexa moved into the kitchen and started to pound the veal that her father took from the refrigerator and handed her. She smiled when hitting the meat with the wooden mallet relaxed the tension she'd felt all day.

By the time Sadi stopped after school, the entire apartment smelled like a fancy Italian restaurant.

Sadi raised her nose and sniffed. "I'm surprised you don't have more friends dropping in to consult, Tony. Around dinnertime."

The bell rang, signaling that someone was downstairs. The three of them laughed. Alexa pressed the intercom, "Yes."

"Alexa, it's Peter. Can I come up? I was worried when you weren't at school. And Sadi was being all mysterious. Are you all right?"

Alexa hesitated. She wasn't used to anyone except Sadi visiting. "Sure." She pressed the button that released the lock on the downstairs door. At the apartment, she listened to the hum of the elevator. Should she tell Peter the truth, or just say she had some mystery ailment or stomach flu? She found she didn't trust anyone anymore.

When he stepped off the elevator and walked toward her, she realized she was glad to see him. She relaxed. "I guess we can set another plate at the table if you like Italian."

"Women or food?" Peter grinned and squeezed her arm before they came back into the big room that smelled of garlic, sweet basil and oregano, and tomato sauce.

"Either. Both. You hungry?"

"Always. You didn't tell me you could cook."

"I can't. But my father can."

"Hi, Peter," her father said with a grin. "I always cook for twice as many as live here. Funny how many people stop along about dinner time."

"Your reputation has spread."

Alexa found herself listening to Peter's voice, the tone, timbre, any clue. Was this what investigating did to you? Made you suspicious of everyone around you? Made you trust no one?

She looked at Sadi, smearing slices of a loaf of bread with butter and garlic. Sadi smiled and shook her head slightly. She was probably saying she didn't invite Peter.

"He's lonely," Sadi whispered when Alexa got close to her, pretending Sadi needed help with slipping the loaf of bread back into its foil bag.

"And that's my problem?"

"Nice problem to have, don't you think?"

"I guess. As long as he doesn't make a habit of it."

The next drop-in guest was Blackwood, still in his civvies, still looking very sexy. Less of a surprise. But when Alexa let him into the apartment, she shook her head, suggesting that if he had any information, he share it later.

"I love these impromptu parties," her father said. "I hope you're off duty, John. This Cabernet has breathed about as long as I can wait." He poured Blackwood a glass of the red wine and handed it to him. "This was the place to come when Violet was alive, too. She was the better cook, so we got twice the crowd. Have to settle for my cooking tonight."

"Alexa doesn't cook?" Blackwood looked at her, his eyes teasing. He tipped his goblet toward her slightly before he took a sip.

"I'm learning from the best." Alexa nodded back, trying to decide if Blackwood had come with information that he was going to have to save till later.

Emma slammed back the door of the loft, took one look at the crowd in the kitchen-dining area, and hurried to her room. This wasn't one of her social nights.

Alexa wanted to chase after her and drag her back, but she didn't. When Emma got ready, she'd come out, or she'd eat after everyone went home. She understood. Every party, every impromptu gathering at the Kane's place reminded them all that one person was missing.

"You have suffered a great loss." The words of Madame Maria rang in Alexa's head. And we continue to suffer. Emma hadn't begun to heal from her mother's death, and now she, and Peter, had lost another one close to them.

The thought sent Alexa's eyes in Peter's direction. He had been watching her, maybe trying to read her thoughts. Maybe jealous of John Blackwood who looked like competition for Alexa's attention.

"Are you old enough to drink?" she teased, pouring him a glass of the wine, remembering he had refused liquor earlier on at the disastrous party.

"On special occasions." Peter took the glass, raised it to Alexa's own. The slight clink broke into the day's mixed emotions, especially the fear and indecision of the afternoon.

Alexa would enjoy the party, gather her wits about her, and get back to work tomorrow. But she'd hope to get Blackwood alone for just a few minutes before he left. She looked at Peter Talbott and John Blackwood side by side. She was keeping mighty fine company these days, regardless of how she had met both of them.

Chapter 17

Alexa woke up the next morning thinking about Peter. He had said goodbye at the door to their apartment, smiled at her, his eyes twinkling, teasing. She wasn't sure how to feel about him. He'd made no move to suggest more than friendship. When they had been dancing at the parties, he'd held her close.

A couple of times she had thought he was going to kiss her, but then he backed off. As if he was either reluctant, scared, or just still making sure what he wanted from her, from their relationship. She guessed that was okay, but he certainly wasn't like other boys she'd dated once or twice, or heard other girls talk about. Most guys seemed to have one thing in mind, and they didn't even hide that.

"Do you like Peter?" Emma asked at breakfast. This was the second time she had asked. Alexa wondered what that meant. Did Emma want her to like Peter, or worry that she might?

"Sure. What's not to like? He's not as pushy as most guys are."

"Hank likes you."

"Bri's brother?"

"Yes. I don't think I'd trust him, though. Bri says he sneaks around their house, surprising her, like a thief or a cautious cat."

"A cautious cat?" Alexa laughed and was pleased that Emma smiled. A smile on Emma's face had been rare of late.

"Emma, did you give Hank my cell number?" Alexa asked, trying not to sound accusing but curious.

"I don't know. I might have. He hangs around, talking to us all the time."

Alexa wasn't sure she liked the idea of Hank hanging around Emma. Why would he want to hang out with fifteen-year-old girls? Unless he was lonely and didn't know anyone else since he'd moved here.

"Do you like Peter?" Sadi asked as she and Alexa hurried to school.

"What is this? Everyone seems to need to know if I like Peter. I don't know. Why does it matter?"

"Hey, don't bite my head off. I was just asking. He seems to like you. He was worried about your not being at school. Maybe he's waiting for you to make the first move. Maybe he's been hurt before and doesn't want to be hurt again."

"Poor baby." Alexa shook her head. "Maybe I'm scared, too."

"I've known for a long time that you're scared of boys."

"Who says?"

"I happen to be very observant."

"I don't see you going out every night."

"I'm too busy. I'll look at men after I get all the degrees I have planned and then get established in my career." Sadi grinned.

"By then you'll be fifty years old."

Was Sadi right? Was she afraid of boys? Of dating? Of Peter?

Alexa tucked the thought away for another time.

Mixing with the crowd trying to get through the doors at Stuyvesant stopped their conversation, but not Alexa's runaway imagination. Maybe she would push Peter a little, see what happened.

Her cell beeped and she grabbed it from her pocket, turning off the ringer. Phones weren't exactly outlawed in the halls, just discouraged. •

"Blackwood, I'm heading to class now. You have my schedule."

"I do. I forgot to tell you earlier, though, that you have an appointment to talk to Marcos Pratt today after school."

"Really? That's great." She got directions to where Pratt was being held and slipped them into her calculus book.

"You're very popular." Peter matched her steps as they headed to class.

"Business." Alexa smiled at him, flirting just the slightest bit. "I need to go to The Orchid tonight. Want to go as my bodyguard?"

"I didn't think you needed one, but now I'm not so sure. Just don't eat or drink anything."

Peter seemed to have her every move, every event, every disaster that happened to her memorized. She guessed Sadi had told him about the weed candy when she wasn't at school. She guess that was okay, but she wished Sadi hadn't mentioned it. And she hated for Peter to think she was so stupid.

"I suppose you would have known not to help yourself to mints on the bar at a nightclub."

"I would. All you have to do is go on the web."

"Where? Weed.candy.com?"

"Probably. Teacher at eleven o'clock." He had sat beside her in class, but now he shut up and turned away.

"Have your homework, Ms. Kane?" Dr. Cassidy was holding out his hand. She hadn't realized he was walking the aisles, double checking that everyone handed work in today.

"Uh, not quite all of it. There's a problem I don't understand.

Do you have any free time today, Dr. Cassidy?"

"I'm supposed to share my coffee break with you because you didn't pay attention in class?"

"That was the day I was ill, remember?"

Cassidy looked around. "Talbott, can you explain anything to Ms. Kane that she missed yesterday and doesn't understand?"

Peter looked at Alexa, never blinking or smiling, totally straight-faced. "I supposed I could give up my coffee break or lunch hour. She'd owe me."

Alexa rolled her eyes. "Not really."

Cassidy turned, and returned to his desk.

The class was long and confusing, since everything was being built on the lesson that Alexa missed. Why hadn't she asked Sadi to catch her up immediately?

The rest of the day was long, and Alexa found her mind wandering.

What was she going to say to Marcos Pratt? What could she find out that no one else could? She'd better try to make a list.

She took the same bus route to the precinct where Bernadette Griffin had been jailed, paying careful attention to everyone at the bus stop, on the bus, around the building. This time, no one seemed to be following her or warning her not to go.

John Blackwood met Alexa at the front desk and the woman who sat behind it recognized her and waved her on. "Marcos Pratt is not your usual street punk," Blackwood said. "Whoever supplies him is either very intimidating, or Pratt is very loyal. We haven't gotten one scrap of information from him."

"Will he go to jail?"

"Maybe. Minimum sentence if he has a decent lawyer. He doesn't even have any priors. See what you can find out, if anything, Alexa."

He showed her to the same room where she had talked to Bernadette. Marcos looked up and smiled as Alexa came in.

"That's better. I'm so tired of those old guys asking me questions. Do I know you? Is this a social visit?"

Alexa smiled back. "It could be. I hear you'll probably be out of here in no time."

"That's more than I've heard. They can't hold me much longer without charging me, though."

"Your lawyer tell you that?"

"I'm a law student. Pays to read up on certain situations before you get in them."

"If you're a law student, why did you resort to dealing drugs?"

"Know how much it costs to stay in college?"

Pratt did look like a straight guy. No tattoos that showed. Clean hair, stylish clothes, although they were wrinkled now. His hair was cut in a conservative style. His fingernails were clean and clipped short. Intense gray-blue eyes studied her. Wouldn't take much for him to look like a lawyer.

"I don't know if you can take the bar exam if you have a record." Alexa kept talking about him without asking specific questions she wanted answered.

"Depends." He smiled. He was through visiting.

"I can get you a break if you give me enough information."

"*You* can cut me a deal? How old are you? Is your daddy a lawyer or a judge? And who sent you to talk to me?"

"Okay, I'll just say you didn't give me any information. Between you and me, I think your keeping your mouth shut is working. But I want one scrap of information. Someone is the head guy for supplying drugs to the New York City high schools. Does The Blue Orchid figure into this supply chain in any way?"

He studied her again. She waited. He smiled. "You like going to The Orchid?"

"Music's good. I hear they have some good live bands lined up for the near future."

"Saturday night. I was looking forward to that. Pyrotechnics on stage."

"Isn't that illegal?"

"Not if they stay with the rules for fireworks as part of their act. Or occasionally pay someone hush money."

"So you recommend I keep going there and keep my eyes open?"

"Wouldn't hurt."

"Who's playing tonight?"

Pratt shrugged. "They don't give out dance programs in here. Need a date?"

Alexa studied his flint-sharp eyes. He met her stare and didn't look away. "Maybe Saturday." She scribbled on her notebook page. "If you're free, here's my phone number."

She stood and walked out, knowing his eyes followed her. There was something about Marcos Platt that she liked. He wasn't a smart ass, he wasn't pushy, he didn't seem to be on anything, or if he was, he wasn't so addicted that he was strung out. If she had met him at school or at a party, she'd have accepted a date.

Keep in mind, Alexa, a little voice inside her said, *there's a reason he's in jail. He's part of a supply chain that puts drugs in the hands of fifteen-year-old girls.*

And that's the reason he might lead me to the head of the chain, she reasoned with herself. She wasn't taken in by him, but there was a fascinating silence about him that she'd like to know more about. She found that she liked quiet people that you had to dig deep to get to know.

You don't know much about Peter. Well, he falls somewhere in between the very deliberately quiet like Marcos and the guy who can tell you all there is to know about himself in half an hour.

Her musings made her shake her head. Blackwood didn't know how to interpret the gesture.

"You didn't get anything else from him? We've found him very cooperative but totally uncommunicative."

"I didn't find out any more than you did. I never met a guy that poised and seemingly sure of himself while he's sitting in jail."

Blackwood laughed. "And how many guys have you met in jail?"

"Well, hey, isn't that what this job is about? Getting some experience with the legal system, above ground and below?"

"Mainly below. You have any leads?"

Alexa shook her head. "How much longer can you hold Marcos without charging him with something?"

"Not long. If we charge him with dealing and he has a good lawyer, he's out of here, too. Frankly, he has us a bit puzzled."

Alexa understood exactly. Marcos Pratt was a very puzzling guy. She found she hoped he'd be free by Saturday.

"I have an idea," Alexa said. "I don't know if you can do this, but since you can't hold him much longer anyway, why not let him out so he can go with me to The Blue Orchid on Saturday. I can keep an eye on him, that night at least, and he might help me get some new information."

Blackwood seemed to think that idea over. Alexa waited. "That just might work on some level. I'll see what I can do about it. But you have to promise me you'll be careful."

"Are you going to worry about me like my father is doing? Do all cops worry about their fellow cops? Is this a well kept secret in cop-dom?"

"Yeah, you're catching on fast. But I trust in your abilities. I promise I won't secretly go along on your date to watch after you."

"Great." Alexa hurried away from the police station. *And I'll see if Marcos really calls me or if he was playing me for a fool.*

Chapter 18

Peter called just as she got to the door of the loft building. Sadi had plans with her parents and hadn't stopped by today.

"You had your cell turned off. Where were you?"

"You want my daily schedule? And is it possible that there are times that I don't want to talk to anyone?"

"Even me?" His voice teased.

"Even you, Mr. Popular. You probably have a dozen other girls you could call."

"Yeah, I do, but I thought you might want to go dancing tonight. If not, I'll call one of them."

Alexa knew a dozen girls would probably be happy if they were number three or even number ten on Peter's list of possible dates. Was she number one? Did that make her feel good?

"If you have to think about it, go ahead and say no. I can take it. I'm tough."

"I don't think you are. I think you're good at pretending. How's your mother doing, Peter?"

There was a pause, and Alexa wished she hadn't put an end to their light bantering. But she wanted to know, and she didn't want to ask him tonight.

"She's having a hard time. But I'm no help to her. Thanks for asking."

"Pick me up at eight?" That would give her a couple of hours to work calculus problems. Or try.

"Will do." He was gone.

Alexa didn't feel like studying. Where was her discipline?

Her father practically met her at the door. "Al, will you check on Emma? She's in her room and I think she's crying."

"And you don't know what to say?"

Alexa never fought with her father, hadn't fought with her mother, but she wished he would be more aggressive with trying to connect with Emma again. Were they ever connected? Alexa had never taken time to wonder or find out before. Their mother connected them all. A machine without the right connecting parts fell to pieces. Was it up to Alexa to reconnect her father and Emma?

She thought of Peter, not knowing what to say to his mother, how to help her. She understood his problem perfectly.

She knocked on Emma's door. There was silence for a minute.

"Who is it?" Emma's voice was shaky.

"Just me. Can I come in?" Alexa didn't wait for a yes. She twisted the knob and walked into Emma's darkened room.

"When did you start asking?" Emma blew her nose.

"You sounded upset. I didn't know if you wanted company." Alexa wandered around the room, looking at all Emma's things so neat in their places. She collapsed into a papasan chair. Rags jumped into her lap immediately. Cats are supposed to be psychic. Maybe Emma had upset Rags, too. Alexa stroked the soft pale fur as Rags pushed her feet into Al's stomach, making a nest.

"Every once in a while, I just miss Lexie so much, I can't deal with her being gone." Emma pulled her feet up and sat yoga style on her bed. She seemed willing to talk.

"Yeah, I understand. I can't imagine losing Sadi. There's nothing like a best friend. Or several, like you have."

"I like Bri and Amber, but things are different. Sometimes they talk to each other and leave me out. Or go someplace without me like they did today. They went off after school without waiting for me."

"I was just thinking about how Mom held our family together. We seemed to be pulling apart without her. Dad looks lost sometimes, and I don't even know what to say to him. Maybe Lexie held you four together, and you didn't even realize it."

"Yeah."

"Are you reading that book, *Les Miserables*? In French, Em?"

Alexa thought if they talked about something else, Emma could catch her breath.

"Yeah. It's harder than I thought, but suddenly it's going smoother than when I started."

"Why would you do that? Read it in French? It's a really long book in English."

Emma stared at her hands, polish chipped, nails ragged. "It's silly, I guess."

"I doubt it."

"Well, when Mom was really sick, I made a promise to God that if He'd let her get well enough to go see the Broadway show of *Les Mis*, I'd read the book in French. She really, really wanted to see the show when it came to New York."

"And I remember we got to go."

"Yeah, she got a lot better all of a sudden. I thought she was going to be all right. I felt sure that God had decided not only to make her better, but to make her well."

What to say? Alexa's faith has slipped a whole lot even before her mom got sick. "I don't think He works that way. Not that He can't do a miracle, but He pretty much leaves our world up to us and the people around us. Why did Lexie die instead of you or Bri or Amber?"

"Cause neither Bri nor Amber took that ecstacy. They pretended they did but they were afraid of it. I took just a little bite and then I got scared."

"Did you approach both Bernadette and Billy Razzi to buy drugs?"

"You found that note in my drawer, didn't you? I knew you were in here snooping." Emma was getting angry, and Alexa decided that anger was a better place than where she was.

"I wasn't snooping. I needed to borrow a little purse for going out. My capri pants don't have pockets. I did take the note and I talked to Billy. I'd like to know where Billy and Marcos Pratt get their drugs. Do you have any idea?"

"Not me. Even finding someone to buy from scared us."

"Good. Stay scared. And no more smoking pot, either."

"I really didn't like it. It made me feel sad."

Alexa warned Emma about the new weed candy. Who knows? It might get circulated at school.

"Pot in candy?" Emma shook her head.

"Just don't eat anything someone offers you if you don't know the person. Or even if you do know them." Alexa handed Rags to

Emma. He was limp like a stuffed toy now and willing to cuddle with her. "I'm going out with Peter. Don't know what time I'll be back."

"On a school night?" Emma smiled.

Alexa laughed. "Yes, on a school night. I'll catch up with homework over the weekend, I promise."

Alexa found herself dressing carefully, taking more time with her hair and her makeup. She tried not to think about what that meant. All this having real dates was new to her. She knew most girls started dating in middle school, so she was a little behind. She'd had other priorities.

She punched in Sadi's number. No answer. Maybe they went out to dinner. Or more likely Sadi had to accompany her parents to visit their friends. They were part of a tightly woven Chinese community in New York, meeting together for meals and to speak Chinese. Sadi had said a long time ago that there was no possibility of returning to China, but they missed some of the old ways, food and drink. Sadi usually tried to get out of going with them, but occasionally she had no choice.

She left Sadi a cryptic message. PETER—BLUE ORCHID—WATCH FOR MESSAGES IF YOU GET BACK AND GET THIS.

Al didn't expect any trouble, but she liked having a backup number besides Blackwood's. And she certainly didn't plan to carry her tracking device lipstick on a date with Peter Talbott. She smiled at the idea.

Peter buzzed below and then came up to her door. She invited him in. Tony handed him a small glass of wine and they talked about jazz and old movies for a few minutes. Peter seemed knowledgeable about everything her father brought up. Alexa was impressed. Most boys his age knew only the latest baseball scores and the name of the most violent or disgusting movie of the week.

"Your dad's a fascinating guy," Peter said as they rode down in the slow, creaky elevator.

"He's wonderful. Thanks for taking time to visit, Peter. I think he has friends coming over tonight, but he's lonely a lot."

Peter called a taxi and opened the door for Alexa. She slid into the backseat and he slid in beside her, suddenly feeling comfortable, as if she'd known him since grade school. She wished she had. He handed the driver a card, then put his arm around Alexa and pulled her close.

They were quiet until the cab pulled up in front of a bar on a back street that Alexa had never heard of.

"I thought we were going to The Orchid."

"Do you mind a surprise? I love this place. They know me here, and it's been a few weeks since I dropped in."

What could she say? He opened the car door, and she stood on the sidewalk while Peter paid the taxi driver. Blue neon sizzled and popped as the tubes spelled out "Born Blue."

"It's a jazz club, or maybe you realized that."

Peter acted as if he hung out in New York City nightclubs all the time. Did he?

The place had dim lights, dark corners, and smelled of cigarette smoke and perfume, not cheap perfume either, but musty, sexy scents. Her eyes had to adjust to realize that most of the patrons were black. Not rappers, but men in suits and women in low-cut dresses that looked expensive. This was no dive.

A murmur followed them across the room to a table in the front.

"Peter, my man, where you been?" The waiter who appeared from the shadows knew Peter. "We missed you."

"Had some bad going down. This is Al, you'll like her. She's never been here, so look after her. She likes red wine and blue notes."

The waiter checked Alexa's ID, the one that said she was twenty-one, then vanished, and reappeared as if he was part-genie. Alexa's Merlot was smooth and had a beautiful red color. She sipped it slowly, needing to keep her wits about her. Peter seemed to think she drank a lot, which wasn't true. Her dad had taught her to handle a glass of wine with dinner, but that was the extent of her alcohol experience.

Another man slid into a seat beside Peter. He was huge and his smile was bigger. Pete, boy, you've been missed. Come on up."

"Will you be all right, Alexa?" Peter said after he introduced the man as Owen something or other. Al was too surprised to hear his last name. He had diamonds on several fingers that caught the light and Al's eye. Were they real?

"I–" Before she could agree or disagree, Peter got up, walked up onto the low stage, and sat down at the piano. His fingers ran up and down the keyboard a couple of times to limber up, then he started an improvisation that the rest of the band followed.

The audience clapped and commented, then got quiet along with Alexa as blue, jazzy sounds filled her with a whole list of emotions. Dreamy, soothing, mellow notes, lost dreams, found joys, deep longing, and last but not least, a sense of awe for Peter.

Chapter 19

For at least an hour, Alexa listened as if she was under some kind of spell cast by Peter and the music. She continued to sip the wine slowly and nibbled on the dish of peanuts and pretzels the waiter had set on the table for her.

Not once did Peter look up, look at her, smile. He, too, seemed to be in some other world, totally transported with the music. Somewhere away from here, the dark room, far away. If he needed to escape, he had.

But he'd left her behind and after a time, Alexa started to fidget. She wiggled her fingers in her lap, tapped her feet without making a sound, then took deep breaths to stay centered.

No one was dancing. Some of the music had a good beat, but no one even moved around the tables. Occasionally someone said, "Yeah, play it," or "Way to go." But the cheerleading was quiet too, almost whispered, reverent. No one near her carried on a conversation, and when she glanced around, all eyes were on the band.

They finished the set with some pieces that she recognized from

Kind of Blue by Miles Davis. The big man who had invited Peter onto the stage played trumpet, taking the lead from Peter, but Peter kept playing piano. Her dad would love this place. Would Peter bring him here, and her, too, of course?

Finally, he came off the stage and sat beside her, smiling. "Sorry, Al. I left you alone longer than I meant. Guess I got carried away. Been a long time since I was here."

"You used to come here all the time?"

"Almost every night."

She wanted to ask if he came alone, but she knew the answer. Of course he did. Bringing her here was special, an act of trust on his part. She didn't have to be psychic to know that.

"Thanks for sharing a piece of you I didn't know existed."

"You knew I played piano, didn't you? You've been to the school jazz concerts."

Alexa swallowed and tried not to look guilty. She didn't want Peter to know she'd gone to the concerts just to watch him play. She'd lie. "No, I don't go out much."

Peter stared at her. Had he seen her at the concerts? Had he caught her lying? "You don't go out at all, do you? I sure don't understand that. I guess I should say thanks."

"We're even." She smiled. "I guess we'd better go, though. I have an early class."

"So do I." He stood, took her elbow, and steered her through tables where people talked now, laughed, ordered more drinks. They spoke to Peter, congratulated him. He nodded, but said nothing.

In the cab home, Peter kept talking. "I started coming here when I was about twelve. Don't laugh, I came in the afternoon. Just happened one day when I was wandering. I didn't see anyone, so

I stepped up on the stage and started to mess with some notes I'd liked at home. The music sounded different here, sort of fit in better than it did in my house. Know what I mean?"

"Yeah, I do." Jazz fit in at her house, but she could think of lots of other music that wouldn't. Emma listened to her own favorite music on her iPod.

"Owen came in one day and when I finished I heard someone clapping. He'd been sitting at a table listening. I didn't even know it. He gave me some tips and pointers and one night, when I was sixteen, and almost legal, he invited me to play with the band. I've been doing it ever since."

"Would you mind if we brought my dad here sometime?"

"I'd like that. I noticed he likes jazz. That's why I thought it might be safe to bring you here."

"Thank you for trusting me. At first I was upset, since I really needed to go to The Orchid, but then I enjoyed the music so much, it was okay."

"You don't keep going to The Orchid because you like the music, do you? At first I thought you were going there because you wanted to go. I thought you were curious." Peter waited.

Alexa didn't know why she didn't tell him everything. She could use his help. But something held her back. Maybe thinking that the fewer people who knew about TIF, unless they were a member of the team, the better. If Alexa and whoever else was working for the police did a good job, the teen police unit would *could* continue. She was sure there'd be other times the police would need teens undercover.

Peter was rich. Cops aren't rich. Was that it? Maybe Peter wouldn't be interested in dangerous work unless it was in his blood. Well, she didn't have to figure out her motives for keeping quiet. She should just enjoy Peter's company. Fortunately, he didn't expect her to chatter all the way home, since that's where they were now. She'd spent the whole trip thinking.

At the door of the loft apartment, Peter took her arm. He stared at her in the dim light. "I wish I'd met you a couple of years ago, Al."

The correct response was why, but before Alexa could speak, Peter's lips found hers. He pulled her closer, deepened the kiss. She returned his passion, surprising herself at how natural this felt. He ran his fingers across the back of her neck, making her shiver. Then through her hair, grasping it to keep her close.

Suddenly he pulled back and took a deep breath. He let it out slowly, warm on her eyelids, her cheeks. Neither spoke. Then he spun around and left before she could say anything, or respond in any way.

She leaned on the door, blinked her eyes, waited until her heart stopped pounding. Why had he left so suddenly? Not knowing, not wanting to guess, she went into the apartment. She was glad her dad had gone to sleep. She slipped off her shoes, then quiet as little cat's feet, she scampered to her room, let herself in, latched the door with only a click.

To her surprise, tears rolled down her cheeks and she feel across the bed, weeping as if her heart would break.

"So, let me get this straight. Peter kissed you and it made you cry?" Sadi questioned Alexa on the way to school the next morning.

"Don't ask me to explain, Sadi. That's just what happened."

"Was the kiss all that bad?" Sadi grinned.

"Of course not. It was just, just, well unexpected?"

"I don't buy that. You knew he liked you."

"You're right. I wanted him to kiss me. And the kiss was all I had hoped for and more. But, this may sound strange, it was almost, well, almost as if he was saying good-bye. The way he turned and almost ran away afterwards."

Both girls walked quietly, thinking about that possibility. Then Sadi said, "Maybe you should be a writer, Al. You have too much imagination for a cop."

"Imagine this, Sadi. At lunch, you sit down and help me finish my calculus homework. Otherwise, I'm in deep you know what. And if I don't keep my grades up, I can't even be a junior cop."

Franklinstein raised his bushy eyebrows when Alexa handed in her homework, as if he didn't believe in miracles. Sadi had even helped Alexa understand most of it, which was the biggest miracle of all.

Peter was absent. His desk sat empty. She breathed a sigh of relief when the class was over. She had no plans for after school. They could go to her place and take a time out. She was badly in need of a time out. When she was a kid, she played tag with the neighbor kids. If you were winded, freaked out, needed to catch your breath, you hollered, "King's X." She didn't know what that really meant, but in the game it meant no one could tag you until you were ready to get back in the game. *King's X*, she said to herself now.

"You want me to go on home so you can be alone with your daydreams and your fantasies?" Sadi teased.

"Since when have you kept me from daydreaming?" Alexa sighed. "What I really need is a hard and sweaty workout. I don't like sitting around, thinking."

"Especially when you didn't see Peter all day."

"How do you know that?"

"Because I didn't either, and you would have mentioned him if you did. You would have told me you started crying and had to leave class, or that he wants you to go watch him play piano again tonight."

"Watching someone do something is usually not my style."

"Exactly. Let's not go home. Let's go to Mr. Chee's and spar. You need me to kick your butt a few times until you settle down to who you used to be. Like the predictable friend you were two weeks ago."

So they did. They waved to the young woman, Chee's daughter, at the desk, hurried to their lockers, suited up, and found an empty room.

Both bowed before they stepped on the matt. Then they bowed to each other. Sadi attacked before Alexa could focus her mind on where they were. She had to bounce back and defend quickly or end up with a black eye or bloody nose. Sadi never held back. She didn't now. She threw Alexa twice before Alexa gained her senses. All her training fell into place and she fought back, yelling at the top of her voice every opportunity she got. Yelling felt good. Bad flew out with the shouts. Energy came back in.

Finally, both felt satisfied. "Draw," Sadi said, bowing to Alexa.

"Who says?" Alexa bowed back. They stepped off the mat and bowed to the center as if Mr. Chee was there himself watching.

"I do. Feel better?"

"Yes, Sadi. Thanks. Most of the time, you know me better than I know myself. Why is that?"

"You were just off center. Now you're in control again, no matter what happens."

"Why did you say that?"

"I just meant in general. I'm not having any psychic visions. Any more dreams?"

"Too tired. Maybe tonight." She hoped not.

They parted at the gym and Alexa hurried home, not allowing herself to think about anything. Peter, this case, Emma, school. A whole weekend stretched before her. And the vibration of her cell signaled her next adventure.

She didn't recognize the number. In fact, it said, "blocked." She decided to answer. "Alexa."

"Where were you? I've been trying to get hold of you all day. Do we have a date tomorrow night?"

It took her a minute to recognize the voice, silky, assured like its owner.

"Marcos, is this you?"

"You told me to call you, didn't you?"

"You didn't have to block your number. I almost didn't answer."

"But you don't know my number, do you?"

"No, that's right. I still wouldn't have known it was you. But I tend not to answer anyone who blocks their number."

"I'll remember that. And Saturday? I'm without wheels. How about you meet me at The Orchid at eight o'clock? You cool with that?"

After last night, she didn't want to go out with anyone but Peter. Then she reminded herself this wasn't a date. This was work.

"Okay, but then I might not come alone."

"What's his name? Is he competition?"

"Sadi. Don't try to compete with her. She's black belt. She just kicked my butt with some very serious martial arts moves."

"Oh, I love aggressive women."

"Your date is with me, remember?"

"Sure. Want me to bring her a guy?"

"No. She'll be fine. I assume if you're calling me, you're not still stuck in a jail cell."

"They couldn't hold me. I knew if I was patient that would be the case. I didn't even have to call my lawyer."

Alexa smiled. But she knew he probably had one on call, and that if she hadn't gotten him out, he would be out anyway.

"Okay, Saturday at eight, ready to dance." Alexa slapped her cell closed and was glad she'd just had a good workout. Never know when defense moves might come in handy. Especially going out with a criminal she hardly knew. Was she losing her mind? Investigating a case? Or was she suddenly becoming a woman she hardly recognized?

Chapter 20

Alexa was jumpy all day Saturday. She and Sadie went to a Tae Kwon Do meet, which lasted until about two o'clock. Alexa preformed badly. Her students did poorly, which she felt was her fault. When she got home, she wanted to crash and burn, sleep the rest of the day, forget she had an eight o'clock date with someone she barely knew. Someone she'd met in jail.

Finally, she admitted she was afraid.

Her dad was in the kitchen, preparing lasagna for dinner. She worked near him for a few minutes, making a salad, setting the table, buttering garlic bread to put in the oven at the last minute.

"Okay, what's wrong, Al? You worried about tonight?" After placing the dish of lasagna in the oven, her father wheeled around and faced her.

Alexa bit her lip and continued placing silverware by plates. "I guess I have to admit I'm scared." She had already told her father she was going back to The Blue Orchid with Marcos Platt. He hadn't been too happy about the date, but he understood.

"It's all right to be afraid, Al. I was afraid lots of times when I was a cop on the streets. You'd be crazy not to be."

"So how do you deal with it?"

"You walk through it. Acknowledge it and go on."

Alexa knew what her father would say. She just wanted to hear it again. She bent over and gave him a hug. He held her tight for a few seconds. "Is it going to be hard for you to head up TIF with your own daughter on your team?"

"Of course it is. But I'm proud of you, Al. I'll be proud of your work. I am already. You're the only one really staying on top of this investigation."

"How about John?"

"Blackwood? Yes, he's with you, but most of the time he has more cases than he can handle. We all did when I was on the street. You deal with the one that demands the most attention."

"I'm free to concentrate on just this one thing."

"Yes, which makes your investigation especially important. Remember the old TV show that sent cops on the street every day saying, 'Be careful out there'? Be careful out there, Al."

"I will, Dad. I will."

Alexa didn't eat much dinner. She took her time getting ready to go out. She didn't have many dressy clothes, only cargo pants and knit tops or T's. She felt she didn't need to be dressed up tonight, but she wanted to look nice, nicer than school clothes. So she went back to the form-fitting capri pants and a burgundy top that flattered her. She took a little more time with makeup, using some mascara. She twisted her hair into a loose knot on top of her head, letting little pieces fall as if she had been careless putting it up.

She thought that was a style now, looking disheveled on purpose.

The idea made her smile.

"You go, girl," she whispered. "Remember you're a cop tonight."

Hearing Sadi talking to her father, she grabbed her small purse with the chain, slung it over her shoulder, and opened her door.

"Hey, lovely lady," her father said. "I'd be proud to be with you, either one of you, both of you. Maybe I can tag along."

"That might be a little obvious, Dad." Al bent and kissed him on the cheek, then gave him another hug. "My date would be jealous."

They waved and left the apartment. Outside, Sadi said, "Do you think Marcos Pratt has any emotions, Al?"

"Yes, but I think he's one of those guys that prides himself on not showing his feelings. He was really cool sitting there in jail. As if that was an everyday occurrence for him."

"Maybe it was."

"No, Blackwood said that was his first arrest, and that one didn't stick. He's careful. He got caught this time only because Bernadette was scared. They probably told her they'd be easy on her if she told who supplied her with drugs."

They hailed a cab that swerved right up to the curb. The driver wasn't Ralph. Alexa didn't know this driver. "Where's Ralph tonight?" Part of her resented the fact that Ralph might be looking after her, part of her felt glad for the help.

"His wife is sick. Pretty bad, I think." The cabbie looked in his rearview mirror at Alexa and Sadi. "He may be off for a few days, looks like."

Alexa nodded, glad for the information. If she didn't see Ralph soon, she'd ask her dad to get in touch with him. Her dad kept a connection, however loose, with every cop he'd ever known.

So many of New York's cab drivers were new to the job, many

didn't speak much English, but for some reason, in SoHo, the same drivers stuck around.

"You sure you want to go in there alone?" the driver asked, stopping in front of The Blue Orchid. "Looks as if it might be a pretty wild place." Had Ralph put out the word to all his cabbie friends to look after her and Sadi while he was gone?

"We're fine. We have dates meeting us here." As if having a date was any protection. Alexa smiled and tipped the new driver enough so he'd remember her. "You might cruise around here in two or three hours if you don't have a fare," she said.

"I'll try." He pulled away from the curb, leaving Alexa and Sadi standing on the sidewalk.

"We're going to be here three hours?" Sadi grimaced. "I'll be deaf or nutty."

"I'm pushing this case tonight, Sadi. I know something is centered here. I'm going to look around."

"Okay, I'm with you."

The Orchid was jammed with dancers, drinkers, people hanging around watching. The place was more crowded than they'd ever seen it, probably because of the live band who advertised fireworks as part of their act. Alexa thought pyrotechnics had been outlawed on stage in crowded nightclubs after a couple of deadly fires, but like Marcos said, someone had probably paid off the authority who okayed nightclub acts, if there was such a person or bureau.

How was she going to find Marcos? Hang out and let him find her, she guessed. They wove through bodies that circled the dance floor. How could anyone dance, pushed up against each other like they were?

But the techno metal music was electric and people wiggled, arms over heads, smiles big, laughter blending with the loud blasts of what stood for songs. She had to admit that the beat filled her and made her feet want to move. And when she listened carefully, she could hear some cool riffs from the drummer leading the band's way.

To her surprise, across the room, she spotted Hank Sasa. He had already seen her. He nodded and smiled. Something about his being here felt wrong. Was he following her? "Hurry, I don't need Hank Sasa screwing up this night."

"Who?" Sadi asked.

"Hank, Brianna's stepbrother. I swear he's following me. And he seems to always know where I am or where I'll be."

"That's a little creepy, Al," Sadi agreed.

"Cokes," Sadi said when they finally got to the bar.

The cute bartender smiled as if ordering Cokes said they were sissies or newcomers to the scene. No way was Alexa going to drink any alcohol tonight. She needed her wits about her.

Drinks were frosty and came napkin-wrapped. Alexa paid from her cop fund. Wasn't her expense account going to look strange? Cokes, taxis, bus rides, psychics, and tarot readings. An eclectic mix.

They didn't move far away from the bar, which was a small island with fewer people, allowing them to talk if they stood close.

"Look, Al." Sadi nodded her head toward Alexa's Coke. "Something is written on your napkin."

Alexa peeled off the paper, now soggy. Because the words were blurred, they read with more of a creepy context. BE CAREFUL. She looked back at the bar. The cute guy was even busier and didn't look at her. She didn't think she'd ever seen him before.

She turned back around only to bump right into Marcos Pratt.

"Noisy, isn't it? Hope you didn't want to talk so we could get to know each other better." His smile was wicked and his blue eyes sparkled.

"I know where there's a quiet piano bar." Alexa smiled back, remembering her date with Peter. How different this night was.

Alexa started to introduce Marcos to Sadi, but he was already steering her toward the dance floor. She handed off her drink, not even sure it was Sadi who took it from her.

They didn't really dance, just stood close and moved their hips. Someone pushed her, and Alexa found herself in Marcos's arms. She stepped back as much as she could. His eyes teased. Then he pulled her to the other side of the dancers, right up against the far wall.

Leaning on it, pinning her in front of him, he smiled. "You look out of place here, Alexa Kane. Why did you agree to meet me here?"

Alexa couldn't see how she looked out of place. "I look pretty much like all the other women here,"

He shook his head slowly. "Not true. If you did, I wouldn't have showed up. Want to leave?"

"No, the band's good. I hear there are fireworks later."

She was thinking she'd made a mistake, though. How was she going to get away from Marcos to look around the building a little more? She wanted to go upstairs, in the back. She didn't know what to look for. Anything. Whatever was suspicious or out of place.

A man helped her get free. "Pratt. You're wanted upstairs."

Marcos looked at Alexa. "Don't get lost, promise? Or go off with someone else. I'll find you again."

Alexa nodded and watched him leave. Why was he going upstairs?

What was happening there? This was her chance. She wiggled back to where she'd left Sadi, hoping she was still there. She was, talking to a guy, but aware that Alexa was coming toward her. Sade smiled up at the man, excused herself, and led the way toward the restrooms.

"There was a good possibility of my never finding you again. Where's Marcos?"

"Someone came to get him. I saw a door by the restrooms the other night. Let's see where it goes."

Alexa looked around, eased the door open, then grimaced, feeling foolish. Storage, cleaning supplies, stacks of soft drinks, boxes of liquor and mixes. Furniture polish fumes, oily rags, dust.

"Good start." Sadi grinned. "We know where we can get a broom if we need one."

They crossed in front of the bar again. The cute bartender was gone. Alexa wondered who he was. Fortunately, she hadn't seen Hank Sasa again. Was he still here?

In the opposite hall, next to the men's room, which sent far from desirable odors their way, was another door. Alexa looked around and opened it quickly.

"Stairs. Come on, Sadi." She pulled Sadi through the opening and closed the door quickly.

The lighting was dim, but got better as they neared the second floor of the old building. Dust, mold, the ancient stairway testified to the fact that the building had stood for many years.

Sound was muffled by the walls, but not enough to keep the beat of Alexa's heart and nerves from echoing the drums from the hard rock. Once or twice the ancient stairs creaked, but no one would ever hear their approach if anyone was on the second floor.

The door opened onto an L of halls. One led into darkness, the second into shadow then some light from what might be an office.

Alexa and Sadi, backs to the wall, slid along, staying alert. Alexa reached out, stopped Sadi, and peeked around the corner of a plate glass window.

Inside, a number of men sat around a table, smoking, drinks beside them, paperwork scattered. Quickly, Alexa studied each face for one that was familiar. Her eyes stopped at Marcos Pratt. She winced, feeling as if he knew she was there, even though his face showed nothing.

One man with his back to her looked familiar, but she couldn't see his face. And the third, she tried to place. She'd seen him in the newspaper. She breathed, ran through her mental files, then it came to her. The third man was a very outspoken member of the city council. Just last week she'd seen a photo of him getting some kind of an award.

The Blue Orchid was a legitimate business. This could be a legitimate business meeting about nightclub profits, which bands to schedule next, that sort of thing. But Alexa had a gut feeling that wasn't the case. They wouldn't meet at night, but during the day. Unless the city councilman couldn't get away. Her mind was running a million miles an hour when Sadi tugged on her arm.

Sadi hadn't been studying the men like Alexa had. She'd apparently been studying the layout of the upstairs. "Down there, past this room, I think there'd be an office," she whispered. "If there's an office, there would be records. We could hack into their computer."

Alexa nodded her agreement. She and Sadi got down on hands and knees and crawled near the wall and below the huge plate glass window. As soon as they were past it, they stood and skipped to the next door.

Sadi eased it open, peeked in. Sure enough, there was a desk, a couple of computers, three file cabinets. There was almost no light, but the computer screen would light up. Why hadn't Alexa brought a flashlight? *And where would you have put it?* She almost giggled thinking about the outline of a flashlight in her tight pants or even in her tiny purse. And her cell filled her purse, that and her mirrored lipstick, not turned on, a fold of bills, a tissue. No help right now.

Sadi shoved Alexa gently toward one computer; she took the other. As soon as the screen lit up, both girls started searching for programs, passwords, any way to get information.

They hadn't worked long when they heard the meeting next door breaking up. The walls were thin and the men loud, laughing, coughing, snorting, the noises that men make, especially older men.

Turning off the computers reluctantly, Alexa and Sadi ran to stand behind the door in case anyone decided to come inside. Then what will you do, the voice inside Alexa's head asked. *Smash and run. Push and run. Duck and run. Don't let anyone see who you are.*

Instructions flew through her head, but she didn't have to use them. Within a couple of minutes the hall was quiet.

"You go back to work, Sadi. You're a better hacker than I am. I'm going to check around in the hall, or go in their meeting room. See if I can spot any clues as to what the meeting was about."

"Be careful."

"I will. Let's say fifteen minutes, then we'd better show up again downstairs. Marcos will be looking for me."

"It will look as if we're coming from the men's room." Sadi giggled.

"Shut up. We'll think of something."

"Yeah, you followed your date." Sadi booted up her computer again.

Alexa slipped out of the office door, glancing in both directions. She didn't hear any voices, any footsteps, anything except her own heart pounding. Could anyone else hear that booming?

She entered the bigger meeting room quietly, although it was empty. No files stood against the walls. Nothing was in the room except the meeting table, and it was bare. There weren't even any wastebaskets. Carefully, she slid back into the hall.

She tiptoed to the corner, to the unlighted hallway. She couldn't see more than a few feet into the cool shadows. All the while, the music seeped into the soles of her shoes through the floor, filling her with the strangest scent of fear. *Walk thought the fear. Walk through the fear.*

She let those words accompany her into the darkness, her hands creeping along the wall. If there was another room down here and someone was in it, wouldn't light be seeping from under the door?

No one was here. She might as well go back and help Sadi, or leave Sadi here trying to get information while she hurried back downstairs to look for Marcos.

She had almost made that decision when someone grabbed her arm, opened a door beside her, shoved her inside.

"Hey!" Her protest echoed through the room and as her own voice faded out, she heard the tiny snick of the doorlock. She caught her balance, ran back to the door, twisted the knob. Nothing.

Someone had locked her in the dark room.

Chapter 21

Alexa tried to push down her panic. *Think. Think. Calm your mind.* She tried to remember everything Mr. Chee had said about inner calm, outer calm, power, focus.

At the same time, she wanted to scream and kick at the door with no mind at all, just pure panic and fear.

She looked around. The room was empty. No table, no chair, no desk, nothing. The space had a hollow, empty feel as bare rooms do. The floor was indoor-outdoor carpet, she guessed, thin and useless as far as something that would help her break out.

She took deep breaths. She closed her eyes and took more deep breaths. She opened her purse and took out the lipstick, twisted the second band, turning on the tracking device. Someone would know she was still at the club. She twisted the doorknob again, thinking this might be a prank or a bad dream. The hard, cold metal was rigid. Unmoving.

Who? Marcos? Don't go there. Anyone could have locked her in. Hank Sasa was in the club, had been watching her. Could he be connected to all this drug mess in some way? Was he lying about why he came to New York to live with his dad? Anyone could have seen her and Sadi in the hall, watching the meeting going on. The bar had bouncers. She suspected that people working for The Orchid cruised the crowd looking for problems before they happened.

They'd look for drunks, under-age kids who had slipped in but might threaten the club's liquor license. Did whoever ran the club pay the cops to turn a blind eye to all the club's activities unless there were problems?

Someone thought Alexa was a problem. The same someone who had forced her inside his car and threatened her?

All the thinking helped her to calm down. She grasped the doorknob and pushed against the door, testing the thickness. The door was old along with the building. The wood seemed to give just a little.

Her leather flats weren't exactly good shoes for kicking, but what choice did she have?

She closed her eyes, focused her energy, balled her fists, leaned back. Her foot flew forward, and she yelled at the same time. "Aiii!"

The impact landed her on her butt, which hurt nothing but her dignity. She could both see and hear Mr. Chee laughing.

She gathered her strength again. Kicked. The door splintered. Again! She ignored the ache in her foot and slammed again through the crumbling wood. Her momentum carried her out the door and into a waiting pair of arms.

She struggled, kicked out, punched as he managed to hang onto her.

"Hey, hey, calm down. You're going to kill off your rescuer if you're not careful." The steady voice, the muscled arms, the male scent belonged to Hank Sasa.

Alexa brushed herself off, took a few more deep breaths, assessed the damage. A sore foot, scratched arms, which she could only feel in the darkness of the hall, and bruised dignity.

"Rescue? I kicked the door down. I was out of there when you came along. Where were you when I was panicked?" *And did you lock me in there in the first place*? she said to herself.

"You didn't act panicked to me. You don't seem panicked now."

The smell of smoke stopped the useless argument. Alexa grabbed Hank's arm. "That's smoke. A lot of smoke. Where's it coming from?"

"Probably just leftover from the fireworks."

Alexa took a deeper breath and coughed. "No, that's not explosive powder or sulfur. That's wood burning."

Hank paused, sniffed the air again, all the while holding tight to Alexa's arm. "I think you're right. Let's get out of here."

"Wait a minute. What are you doing here tonight? Have you been following me, calling me? Are you working with Marcos?"

"It's a long story. You'll get some answers later. Right now we need to find a way to escape or else become crispy critters."

His voice was that of reality, and it had a take-charge tone she hadn't heard before. The poor me, feel-sorry-for-me computer nerd was gone.

She came to life. "You're right. We're wasting time standing here. We need to get out."

"Good, come on." He pulled her toward the staircase.

"No, wait. Sadi. We have to get Sadi."

"Where is she? Were both of you up here snooping?"

Alexa wanted to say she was working. That snooping was what she came here to do. But she wasn't willing to share anything with Hank about her job.

"She's in the office, at a computer."

Hank took off back toward where Alexa had left Sadi. Alexa twisted the doorknob. The room was also locked. "Sadi! Are you still in there, Sadi?"

A noise on the other side of the door said yes, Sadi was trapped the same as Alexa had been.

"The door is locked!"

"Stand back, Sadi." Hank hit the door with a muscled shoulder and it gave a little, but breaking down a door wasn't as easy as the movies made it look.

"Together." Alexa leaned back to kick just as Hank slammed his body against the door.

Both of them spilled into the room, rolling on top of each other, then into Sadi.

"That's pretty graceful, guys." Sadi's voice was totally calm and rather sarcastic. "What's going on?"

"The place is on fire." Alexa jumped to her feet

Sadi's tone said the words she muttered had to be Chinese swear words. A smile flew across Alexa's face, but then she remembered what they were doing there in the first place.

Sadi, reading her mind, patted her pocket, then placed Alexa's hand on her hip. Alexa felt the small square that suggested a computer disc. "Good work," Alexa whispered.

"Can we stop visiting and get out of here?" Hank ran back toward the stairs.

Alexa grabbed Sadi's hand and pulled her along the hall, still dim but already filled with flickering light that suggested flames below. The pounding drums and ear-shattering music was quiet. Yelling, shouting, screams came through the floor.

At the bottom of the stairs, Hank flung open the door. Flames shot into the opening, fed by the air and passageway formed by their leaving the top door open.

The trio spun around and fled back up the stairwell onto the second floor.

"Is there another way out of here, in the back?" Alexa pushed down the idea that the flames were racing up the stairs toward them like some starving animal.

Hank hesitated. "Surely there is, but I've only used those stairs. He swung around and ran into the darkness of the hall.

Smoke drifted, sending gray, acrid ghosts into the upper part of the building. Alexa could hear the roar of the inferno below them. The floor felt hot, even through the soles of her shoes.

"This old building is so dry. Perfect kindling," Sadi said. "I think it's going to blow up fast."

"Are there any windows?" Alexa yelled, then stopped short of running into Hank's arms again.

"Not back here. No doors either. Back to the office or the meeting room."

They spun around, reluctant to go back to where the fire licked under the door they had closed at the top of the stairs.

A plate glass window in the hall looked down at the nightclub. The floor below them was a pit of flames. Alexa could see kids pouring out of the building, crowds gathering. She heard the whine of sirens. No fire crew could help her, Sadi, and Hank if there were no windows.

"The large meeting room had windows but they looked like plate glass and probably don't open. Let's go see if we can break them out." Inside the room she tested the glass. The surface seemed inches thick.

"I don't think so." Sadi led the way. "Let's go next door to the office I was in."

"Hank, you check the end of this hallway." Alexa followed Sadi into the computer room. Her eyes had adjusted to the dim light. Enough to see the walls were solid and bare of office-type decoration as well as windows.

Hank yelled in the doorway. "Down here. There's one window and I think that's a fire escape outside."

The window was there. It should open, but with all of them tugging after they'd spun the lock, it didn't budge.

"Painted shut a long time ago." Sadi took a breath so deep that Alexa could hear her let it out. "We can't break it safely."

"A chair. There are straight chairs in that meeting room. Old-fashioned hardwood chairs made to last." He dashed away from them.

Alexa and Sadi stood together. "What is he doing here? Why is he helping us?" Sadi asked. "Who locked us in? They didn't mean for us to get out."

"Not right away. But maybe they didn't expect the building to catch on fire, either."

"Are you sure? True, the band had fireworks, but someone could have set the fire deliberately, blaming it on the band."

"I don't know, Sadi. I don't know anything. Where is Marcos Pratt? Hank Sasa must have seen us go upstairs. I'm going to accept his help and ask questions later."

Hank carried the straight-backed chair, but Alexa could see it was heavy. "Let's two of us swing it. We'll get more momentum and power that way."

Sadi stepped to the side while Alexa and Hank grabbed a chair arm each. She counted. "One, two, three."

On three, Alexa and Hank struck the glass with the chair, holding on so as not to lose it should the first strike not break the glass enough.

The window cracked, but didn't break. The old building might be kindling for a fire, but it had been built to last, right down to the windows.

"Again," Hank said, counting himself this time. "One, two, three."

A resounding crash following by the tinkling of glass breaking and falling to the floor let in a rush of cool air. Hank pushed Alexa back and kicked out the remaining shards that would rip them like knives if they went through the splintered glass.

He stepped out onto the fire escape first, then reached in to help Alexa and Sadi out. Both pretended they needed help.

"Some days are more of a challenge than others," Sadi quipped.

They all laughed, glad to be outside, then grabbed a rail as the old fire escape groaned and swayed.

"I'll go first to see if it holds my weight," Hank offered. "I don't think it reaches all the way to the ground."

"That figures," Sadi said again.

"Just go, Sadi. My sense of humor vanished a long time ago."

"That's a pity." Sadi stepped gingerly onto the first step. Again the stairway creaked and swayed, but held.

"Should I wait until you're off of it?" Alexa looked behind her to see flames in the hallway. Far enough away not to panic, but how long until the building exploded into one big outdoor barbeque?

"I think we're all right," Sadi yelled back up. "Hank is at the bottom stair."

"How far to jump?"

"Maybe six, eight feet."

"No problem. Here I come." Alexa took the first step, the iron frame of the stairs lit by approaching flames.

She scampered down the stairs, waited until Sadi jumped, then leaped off, landing with an "ooomph" and falling into Hank's waiting arms.

"Let's go," he said, pulling Alexa toward the street, away from the building.

"Okay, but I need to go around front first." Alexa looked at Hank. In the dim light she could see his eyes were warm and smiling, enjoying the adventure they had shared now that they were safe. "Hank, thanks. Leave right now. We don't need your help from here." If someone came looking for her, Marcos or a cop, she didn't want to be with Hank.

"But Alexa, how–" Sadi took Al's arm.

"Go on."

Hank gave her arm a squeeze. Then he vanished into the shadows down the opposite side of the alley.

"I don't think it was a coincidence that Hank was here, watching us. You think he's on our side?"

"We'll talk later, Sadi. Let's go see if anyone needs help, and I want to see if Blackwood is here. I suspect he is. Trust him with that disc, Sadi. He can do more with it than we can."

"You're the TIF person. I'm just along for the ride. And the dash from the burning building, not to mention the scramble down the shaky fire escape."

Alexa was glad for Sadi's sense of humor that held up even when they could indeed have become "crispy critters."

They circled to the front of the building where all was chaos. People screaming with fear and pain, girls crying while being held tight by dates. Onlookers whose awed faces reflected the fire. Flames leaped a couple of stories above the old warehouse. The entire structure was roaring and crackling, sending sparks into the night sky. The earlier fireworks were multiplied a hundred fold.

"Alexa," a voice behind them called. "Are you all right?" John Blackwood took hold of Alexa's arm, held her away from him and looked her over. "You were inside when the fire broke out, weren't you? I knew it. You could have been trampled by the frightened mob. A lot of people were."

"Actually, I was upstairs when the fire broke out. We have something for you. Sadi was able to hack into the computers here and I think you may be able to use the information she downloaded for you."

Sadi handed over the disc. "Glad to be of service."

Blackwood took the disc and placed it in his pocket. "Good work. Let's get out of here." Blackwood pulled them out of the crowd and toward the street. "Your father is going to be frantic, and looks as if you've given me some work to do."

"Wait." Alexa turned, thinking she saw a familiar shape.

"What is it?" Blackwood asked. "Was Marcos Platt with you?"

"Only at the beginning of the evening. Then he disappeared. My guess is that he took off."

"Who did you see?" Sadi was more perceptive, watching Alexa search the crowd.

"No one. I just thought I saw someone I knew."

The person Alexa saw was the man whose back was turned to her when she looked in the window of the conference room. He looked familiar, but no name would come. Billy Razzi? She'd have to think about it.

"Okay, I'm ready to get out of here. I feel guilty not staying and helping where I can, but–"

"That's what the professionals are for," Blackwood assured her. "We've got several fire departments here, medics, and a score of ambulances. You've done enough."

Alexa felt an overwhelming exhaustion. The idea that she'd done enough multiplied into the fact that she'd done too much tonight. Mentally, physically, emotionally, she was used up, a ragdoll with no stuffing of any kind. A cowardly lion, a tin man with no brain, a scarecrow without a heart.

She let Blackwood lead her to his cop car. Then she started to weep softly, leaning into Blackwood, who hugged her and made soothing noises like you'd use for a baby.

Alexa wasn't a baby by any means, but the idea of being cared for had such appeal she gave over to everything she'd held back for the last couple of hours.

Chapter 22

Before they could leave, a couple of cops came over to the car and talked to Blackwood in a low voice.

"Sorry, Alexa, Sadi. You either have to wait for me, and I don't know how long that will be, or find another ride. Your choice." John Blackwood got out of the police car and hurried away with the two policemen.

"I don't want to sit here and wait," Al said, recovering a little. She tried her cell but got no signal.

"How are we going to get home?" Sadie asked. "No taxis are going to be cruising by this mess."

The pair got back onto the sidewalk and watched the inferno for a few minutes until they stopped shaking at their narrow escape. Alexa felt as if she'd fallen during a sparring match a dozen times. Her legs ached, her foot hurt. She was angry and frustrated. She wanted to know what had happened here? Did the band's fireworks set the club on fire, or did someone set the fire and plan to blame it on the band?

"We can walk a few blocks. Surely we can get a cab nearby."

"It's not a very good neighborhood." Sadi followed Alexa, but Al knew she wasn't sure the idea of walking was a good one.

One block away from the fire the streets grew dark. The roar of the fire, voices calling and shouting, noise from the fire blurred. Sadi was right. This was not a place you wanted to stroll, a place you wanted to linger in for even a few minutes.

A big dark car cruised by. Rap music blared from the car speakers so loud you could practically see the car shaking. "Hey, ladies, you coming from the fire? Need a ride?" Laughter almost competed with the music.

"No thanks." Alexa squeezed Sadi's hand, ready to run and pull her along. She was surprised when the car sped away.

The streets became empty, too empty. All the buildings were boarded up. Sadi was right. Certainly no cabbie would cruise here for a fare. Not even the one they'd asked to come back. Once he heard about the fire, he'd stay miles away.

"Should we go back?" Sadi kept looking around, behind them, to each side, wanting to see trouble before it saw them.

"Probably be wise." But Alexa's anger had replaced fatigue and even fear. More and more she knew what had happened tonight was no accident. And someone meant for her and Sadi to die in that fire.

The car pulled up beside them quietly. Both girls jumped back as a male voice spoke. "I figured you'd be here tonight. What are you doing in this neighborhood?" Peter wasn't smiling. "Get in the cab before I have to pick up the pieces."

"We were looking for a cab." Alexa got in, but then transferred her anger to Peter. "We'd have found one in a minute."

"I doubt it. These deserted buildings go on for blocks. I had to pay in advance to get this guy to come down here." Peter nodded toward the cab driver who was making good time getting away from the dark streets.

"I never saw them when we came here before." Of course she had seen them, but she didn't want to admit it to Peter.

"You either weren't looking or you came from another direction. But no way you choose is safe for walking. How'd you get to The Orchid?"

"Cab. But we couldn't exactly call for another."

"Where's your cell?"

"Dead down here. Or my battery is."

"I thought you were a Girl Scout. Be prepared, all that." He turned and, losing his anger, grinned at Alexa.

"I wasn't exactly prepared for the club to go up in flames."

"Where's your date?"

"Sadi and I went alone." Alexa looked over at Sadi, although she knew Sadi wouldn't contradict her. "We don't have to have a date to go dancing. There are always plenty of guys there alone who want to dance."

"I heard you had a date with Pratt. Where is he?"

Was Peter jealous? And how did he seem to know all of Alexa's business. "How'd you hear that? Were you there, spying on me?"

He laughed. "I stopped by for a few minutes. Too crowded." He leaned around Alexa. "You okay, Sadi?"

"On some level. I don't think I want to do that again any time soon. You think the band's fireworks show set the building ablaze that fast?"

"Doesn't take much. The building was old. The stage they were on was wood."

"I hope everyone got out." Alexa sat quietly, but something was nagging at her. Some idea, some thought.

"Thanks for the ride, Peter," Alexa said as she and Sadi got out at the loft. "That was thoughtful of you to think we might still be there and need a ride home."

"No problem." Peter smiled and waved at the driver to go on. Alexa stood watching the cab disappear.

"Problem?" Sadi had planned to stay the night at Alexa's.

"No, I'm just glad he came along. But I can't help but feel he's spying on me."

"He's jealous." Sadi laughed. "He likes you."

"I guess."

Her father had waited up for them. "Thank God you're safe, Al. I heard about the fire. Then the police scanner went nuts with calls."

Alexa hugged her dad. "But Blackwood called you, didn't he?"

"Yes, he told me you were out and okay. Did he bring you home?"

"He'd planned to, but got called away. Peter happened along just in time. We wanted to get out of there. Is anything on the news? Did anyone get hurt in the fire?" Alexa headed for the TV set and clicked it on. News cameras were all over the disaster.

They watched for a minute as beams fell, crashed into the flames engulfing the building, which the fire trucks seemed to be letting burn.

"Why are they just letting it burn?" Sadi asked.

"Too dangerous to try to save it. They'll concentrate on keeping it from spreading." Tony looked at Alexa. "Lots of old buildings down there like that one."

Alexa looked at Sadi. They knew.

"Should you call your parents?" Alexa asked Sadi.

"They think I'm here with you. No sense worrying them."

"I wish we had a copy of that disc you gave Blackwood," Alexa said as they headed for her room and fell onto the bed. Or Alexa fell into bed. Sadi grinned, held up another disc, and sat at Alexa's computer.

"You did!" Alexa sat up and dragged a stool up beside Sadi. Tired as she was, she'd rather see what they could find out than try to sleep.

Numbers, numbers, numbers. No names. Letters suggested the name of people who were involved with the numbers.

"Is it in code?"

"I don't think so. Except these letters and these small numbers correspond to something. Shipments? Sales? Dealers? They've been careful not to actually use a name. At least as far as I can tell. I didn't read all of them. I knew I was running out of time, so I just downloaded the whole file."

Fatigue helped them get bored quickly. Sadi kept scrolling forward and shaking her head.

"Let's look at it again tomorrow. Or call Blackwood and see what he has figured out."

Alexa fell asleep the minute she changed clothes and lay down. But a couple of hours later she came awake.

The back that she saw through the window. That was what her mind was trying to tell her. She knew that back.

A *very fine back indeed.*

Chapter 23

When Alexa woke the next morning, smelling of smoke and needing a shower, she couldn't believe she had slept. Look what total exhaustion will do for you. Her discovery should have made her lie awake, but that hadn't been the case.

"Sadi, Sadi, wake up. I have this awful idea."

"Again?" Sadi rolled over and checked her watch. "It's only six o'clock. Let me get another hour of sleep."

"You can't. You have to listen to what I think."

"Listen to you think?"

"Sadi, you are not even close to being awake. I'll bring you a cup of coffee. You can sleep until then."

Alexa pushed a drowsy Black Bart aside and scrambled to her feet. Pulling on a robe, she hurried into the kitchen. The smell of fresh roasted and filtered coffee made her feel better. Well, not better in her heart or in her mind. A cup of coffee would give her some energy. She was running on adrenaline, but there was no way she could sleep now that she was up and thinking.

"Al, you're up early. Isn't it Sunday? Someone left a Sunday paper by the door." Her father handed her the front page.

Alexa poured a cup of coffee, creamed it, and sat at the table, spreading the newspaper before her. Sadi could sleep in. She wanted to see what take the reporters had on the fire.

"Total blame on the band," her father said. "You think that's right?"

"No one could prove otherwise. Maybe this was all planned. The drug empire needed to lay low for awhile. They invited the pyro-band, used them to cover their tracks. Surely I wasn't getting that close to the big boys."

"Maybe you were. Or they were afraid someone down the food chain would talk. Pratt gives you his boss. That guy talks. On up and up until you reach the top." Her father rolled over to the kitchen and poured more coffee. "Pratt might have been close to the top."

"I doubt it. I talked to him. He didn't tell me much, but he seemed like a fairly nice guy who'd made bad choices."

"But those bad choices led to someone's death."

"I know. But I have to admit, I liked him, Dad. He said he wished he could start over." Alexa took a sip of her coffee, studied the article.

"Lots of criminals say that, but could they have done so, or even given a chance, would they have made different choices for long?"

"I know you're right. But here's what I can't figure out. Hank Sasa helped us get out of that building. He's been following me, I think. Maybe he likes me, but I keep thinking it's more than that. I had seen Hank earlier in the club. Someone locked Sadi and I both in upstairs rooms. I got myself out, but Hank had come after me. We got Sadi out, then found a shaky, but working fire escape." Alexa hesitated, thinking.

"Hank being there seemed like too much of a coincidence?" Her father's detective mind was ahead of her. "Maybe he locked you in and then pretended he didn't, but got you out? Covers his tracks."

"Yes, but I've felt as if he was following me ever since I took this job. He just makes me nervous, but then, a lot of things have made me nervous. Is that normal?"

"You'll feel better when you get some experience under your belt. Never hurts to be cautious, and never trust anyone until you're sure. But remember, you can quit any time you want, Al. I don't want to force this on you before you're ready."

"I thought I was ready." Alexa stared at her coffee.

Sadi staggered in to where they sat. "Where's my coffee? You lied, Al."

"Dad reminded me it was Sunday, Sadi. I was going to let you sleep." Alexa jumped up, found Sadi's cup, and poured it full of coffee, black.

Sadi grabbed it and blew across the top, sipping carefully. "Too late. I'm awake. Sort of. Enough to remember what happened last night wasn't a nightmare, but real. Is it in the newspaper?"

Alexa passed the front page to Sadi. "They're totally blaming the band. Going to be an investigation into how they got a permit to have live fireworks. And that will probably be covered up."

"You'll get discouraged many times, girls." Dad spun his chair. "Pancakes or waffles? Sausage or bacon?"

Alexa held onto her news until they were finished eating. But she ate quietly, running it over and over in her mind. She licked syrup off her fingers, and finished off her second cup of coffee.

"I might have some bad news."

"What now?" Sadi looked at Alexa as if she'd had enough.

"Remember, Sadi, how when we peeked in that window that

someone was sitting with his back to us. And remember that I said he looked familiar, even when I saw only his back?"

"Vaguely. Did you remember who it was?"

Alexa bit her lip. Was she crazy? She hoped she was. "I think it was Peter."

"Peter Talbott?" Mr. Kane stared at Alexa.

"I hope I'm wrong. I–I like Peter. He wants to take you to this great jazz club, Dad. He plays piano there sometimes."

"How can you find out?" Sadi asked.

Alexa shook her head. "I don't know. Ask him?"'

"Is he going to tell you the truth?" Sadi asked. "Yes, Alexa, you're right. I'm part of this drug ring that killed my sister. I don't think so."

"Blackwood called me this morning," Dad said. "They're going over that disc you took off the computer."

"We looked at it last night. Only numbers and some code for people, we think. No name that we found. I hate to think we risked our lives for nothing."

"I don't think that's the case," her father said. "You put a lot of pressure on someone, enough for them to destroy the nightclub that was surely a nice source of income, not to mention a good drug outlet."

"And it wasn't for nothing," Sadi said. "We spotted the city councilman and, if you're right, Peter. Anyone at that meeting was probably at the top of the food chain. Maybe they were all the top dogs. Maybe you should tell the police you recognized Peter. Let them talk to him."

"I don't think I can do that. What if I'm wrong?"

"Then he tells them you were wrong and they let him go." Dad sighed. "You can't depend on anyone to confess they're part of this. Since Lexie died, if we can trace the drugs back to individuals, they can be charged as accessory in her death. That, along with drug dealing, could be twelve to twenty years in prison."

"Peter could be responsible for his sister's death?" Alexa wanted this to all go away. She wanted to go back to bed and wake up with amnesia.

"In a round about way, yes." Her father looked as sad as Alexa felt. "You saw the councilman, Alexa. You'll have to testify that you did, and then the police will have to find the links. Can you say for sure that you saw Peter at that meeting?"

"No, not really."

"I think I'd better go home, Al. Thanks for breakfast, Tony. One of these days my parents want to have you come for dinner."

"I'd like that. Give them my best. I don't know where you were last night." He smiled.

"What are you going to do, Al?" Sadi asked as she got dressed and gathered her things.

"I don't know. "I want to be wrong. But Peter showed up rather conveniently last night. He knew I was at the club with Marcos. He was either following me, or he was there on his own for other reasons."

"You sure have a lot of guys following you these days. Call me when you decide what to do."

"Okay." Alexa lay back down with Black Bart after Sadi left. The big cat purred and cuddled against her stomach. She circled him with both arms and buried her face in his warm fur. He was always there for a hug. Alexa needed a hug.

She slept again for a couple of hours, still tired, frustrated, sad.

She had to do something. All she knew to do was confront Peter, get this idea in her head out into the open. He'd deny any involvement. But she thought she'd know if he was lying.

She got up, showered, dressed carefully, then slipped out of the loft apartment without telling anyone her plan. On the curb, she hailed a taxi and gave the driver the Talbott address.

Chapter 24

Her driver was Ralph, back on the job. He looked at her in the rearview mirror. "I'm glad you weren't in that nightclub fire last night, Miss Kane."

"But I was, Ralph. I was. I was fortunate enough to get out without getting hurt. How's your wife?"

"Better. Much better." Ralph maneuvered around the Sunday traffic, getting her to her destination.

Alexa gave him a better-than-usual tip to make up for all the times she'd ridden with him on her meager allowance.

She stood on the sidewalk looking at the familiar brownstone. Now what? Was anyone home? Was someone looking out a window wondering why she was here? Or waiting for her to come?

Her reason for being there was as thin as gauze, as easy to see through as fog off the river. She rang the bell, her stomach spinning, her heart doing little jump rope skips.

No one answered. She rang again, then waited until she was sure no one was home. Looking back and forth, she slipped into the alleyway and walked to the back. A five-foot wall surrounded the small yard. On a stone patio, pots of late-blooming petunias needed water. In some places, ivy climbed the wall.

With some effort, she was able to jump, grab the top of the wall, and pull herself up and over. She landed in a bed of gravel, narrowly missing other pots of flowers. The crunch of her feet sounded like gunfire. She froze in place, squatting for a minute, ready to fly back up and over.

Anxious feelings deep inside her combined with fairy tales from years and years ago to make her feel she was at the giant's house and he was waiting for her to walk right into his lair. The gingerbread house witch was quietly cackling, her trap set.

Panels of glass in the back door allowed her to peek inside, but the interior was dim. She knocked. Knocked again.

What are you doing?

Visiting Peter.

Why?

What if there's no information on the disc linking him to the drug ring? What if this whole case rides on who we saw at that meeting? On your thinking you recognized his back? No one with any sense is going to list a bunch of dealers on a disc or anywhere else.

If she could find some evidence that linked Peter to this business, them maybe he would talk in exchange for a deal. Peter Talbott would not do well in jail that she knew.

But how was she going to get inside in order to look around? She reached out and twisted the doorknob. To her surprise, the back door wasn't locked. Who left a door open in New York City?

The Little Red Riding Hood wolf. The gingerbread house witch. She had to smile at the way her imagination was running away with her.

Once inside, she sort of remembered the layout of the house.

Bedrooms were on the second floor. There was a back staircase. She found it and made her way upstairs. Here was Lexie's room. She passed it by. Opening the next door, she found the room too sterile to belong to anyone. A guest room. Next, the Talbott's suite, with a bath, sunken tub, closets. A tiny room with toilet. Mrs. Talbott was messy, but that didn't mean they were in town. Just that no one was home on Sunday afternoon.

Peter's room had a faint masculine smell, combined with soap and the slight odor of aftershave. He had showered recently. The bath was humid and a wet towel hung over the shower stall.

Alexa moved to Peter's desk. Middle drawer, pencils, pens, paper clips, the usual desk stuff. Left hand drawer, a file. She rifled through it, not much, some school assignment notes, letters, sheet music, even though Peter seemed to play by ear. Maybe he had once taken lessons. Right bottom drawer, locked.

She grabbed a letter opener from the middle drawer and jiggled the tip in the lock. She looked at the desk top again. Where would she hide a key? Under the lamp base? No. Under the computer keyboard? Nope. A polar bear coffee cup was filled with jelly beans. Alexa stared at it. The cup and candy seemed out of place here. Must have been a gift, maybe from Lexie.

A tiny desk key gleamed from under the cup when Alexa lifted it. She slid it out, palmed it, slipped it into the bottom drawer. When she pulled the heavy drawer out, the key slipped to the floor with a slight click. She stared at the drawer piled almost full with stacks of hundred dollar bills banded together.

"I wish you hadn't done that." His voice was low, in control.

She didn't turn around. "You have so much talent, Peter. What a waste. Why wasn't it enough?"

"There's no such thing as enough money when you have a drug habit. So I thought I might as well make some extra while I was at it."

"You locked me in the room at The Orchid, didn't you?"

"I knew you had seen me in that meeting. And they'd think I had told you everything. You're dealing with some nasty people, Al."

"So are you. Turn yourself in. The police will cut you a deal if you testify against the top suppliers."

"Can you guarantee that?" He stepped up beside her and smiled. She loved that smile. She could have loved Peter. His taking her to hear him play piano was the beginning of his trusting her. "You were foolish to come here alone, Alexa."

"Who says I'm alone?"

Peter hesitated just a little. She made her move. Jumping up, she shoved him. He stumbled and fell over the open money drawer. She was out the door and in the hall before he could recover.

"You can't hide from me in my own house," he yelled as he recovered and dashed into the hall.

"Want to bet?" she whispered, ducking into Lexie's room, sliding under the bed. Next thing she did was slip her cell from her pocket and punch all the buttons on her speed dial. She wasn't going to talk, but that should get someone's attention. She made sure the phone was turned off and lay there, taking deep breaths, feeling dust fill her nose, willing herself not to sneeze.

Alexa felt she'd just learned the most important rule of police work. Knowing when to run, when to hide, and when to call for backup.

He had guessed that she hadn't left the top floor. She heard him in the hall. "Come on out, Alexa. I thought you were a black belt. That you had all these fighting skills. Let's test them."

Sparring in a gym was one thing. Actually taking down someone who was bigger and stronger than you, someone who didn't fight fair was iffy.

They both heard the doorbell. "Shit, you called someone, didn't you, Alexa? Coward." He had narrowed his search while he talked. He stood in Lexie's doorway.

When he bent over and shined a flashlight under the bed, she slid out the other side. Grabbing a gooseneck lamp, she rounded the bed and swung it at him. He had to leap back and that gave her time to run into the hall. But he was fast and grabbed her with both arms around her waist.

She went limp, which surprised him, kicked backward, and almost slipped away. He clutched one wrist. Instead of pulling away again, she grabbed his other arm and pulled him toward her. Her leg bent, she kneed him in the stomach.

"Ooof." He went down and rolled over, but only for a couple of seconds.

Football moves don't always work off the gridiron. Peter miscalculated when he dived after her. All she had to do was sidestep his flying body, let him hit the wall, roll over, then tumble down the stairs. By the time he got to the bottom he was bruised, dazed, and defeated.

Sadi and John Blackwood had turned on every light in the house as they came in. Blackwood and the cop with him had no trouble slipping handcuffs on Peter before he sat up.

"You should have known better than to trust a guy who is that good looking," Sadi said, watching Alexa limp down the stairs.

"Yeah, I've got to get more dating experience. Too easy to fall for a pretty face." Alexa could match Sadi's quips, but inside her heart ached for what might have been.

Chapter 25

By the next Friday night, the case was pulled together, although not totally closed. Tony Kane called a meeting of the Teen Investigative Force to meet at 23 Shadow Street, the Kane loft. This was possible since at this time there were only four members, and one mascot, as Sadi called herself, since she wasn't formally a member of the team. In Alexa's mind, Sadi was as full a member as she was, and if her parents would consent, Sadi could get on the payroll, if there was one. She suggested it to Sadi.

"You mean you're going to get paid for risking your life?" Sadi was in rare form tonight. Maybe it was because Alexa was safe, but Sadi would never admit that she had been worried.

John Blackwood accepted the cup of coffee that Tony poured him. "Black," he said. "No serious cops use cream and sugar." John had watched Alexa spill her cup half full of cream before she added coffee. And she had seen him drink a latte, but she wouldn't tell.

The first big surprise to Alexa was Jacob Collins, the bartender from The Blue Orchid, the one who'd wrapped her Coke in a napkin with the warning, *Careful*. Lot of good it did, since the consequences of snooping had almost cost hers and Sadi's lives.

Jacob had jet black hair and blue eyes, a sexy combination, especially when he smiled and his eyes teased.

"Did you suspect that I was on your side?" he asked Alexa.

"I thought you might be, or just a concerned citizen."

"That, too."

"In case you're wondering, Alexa, Jacob qualifies as a teen. He's nineteen, going on forty," Blackwood said. "We recruited him when we kept hearing rumors of drug dealing at The Blue Orchid."

A knock at the door presented the second surprise. Alexa opened it to Hank Sasa. "Are you still following me?" she blurted out before she could stop herself. "What are you doing here?"

"He's on our team, Alexa." Blackwood shook hands with Hank. "We didn't want to tell you before unless we had to. And, if he'll stay with us, we want to keep him undercover for as long as possible. Hank called us from New Jersey after Lexie died. He asked if he could help. He's been working undercover there for a couple of years."

"How old are you?" Alexa knew the question was rude, but she was so startled, she wasn't thinking about manners.

"I'm twenty." Hank grinned at her. "But I look younger, don't I?"

"It was your story. That your poor mother didn't want you. That you kept being shipped to other relatives."

"Actually, that's true. And I am Bri's stepbrother. But I got over being shoved back and forth between my parents a long time ago. When I turned eighteen, I guess, and could go out on my own. I'm in college part time, heading for Quantico eventually."

"So you took it on yourself to keep an eye on me?" Alexa shook her head.

"Yes, I called and volunteered, since I always liked Lexie Talbott. Not a bad job, looking after you, actually. I enjoyed it, even though I knew I was annoying you."

"Who else is coming here today?" Alexa asked. "Ralph?"

"No, Ralph is just a good ex-cop who has kept in touch with me. He does care about you," Dad said. "I asked him to help when he could."

"I'm just so sorry that Peter Talbott was involved," Alexa said, sitting down again and sipping her coffee au lait.

"We're not. Thanks to Peter's not trusting anyone, we have the information we need to prosecute all the dealers and the top honchos involved in this drug ring." Blackwood laid out paperwork to share with everyone. "We've broken up the largest Ecstasy-related operation in the city's history. And the drug ring bust stretches all over the country. We and other law enforcement people have confiscated eighty-five thousand Ecstasy tablets, 2.5 kilograms of cocaine and three hundred pounds of marijuana. So far. We've got Councilman Rondell Gilner on the federal kingpin statue. He faces as much as life in prison."

Alexa was dumbfounded. "How did Peter help you get this information?"

"I understand what you mean, Al," her father said, following up on Alexa's other statement. "I'm sorry Peter was involved, too. His actions have destroyed his family. It probably never occurred to him that by getting himself involved, he was killing his sister. No one ever gets involved with drugs, thinking about the consequences to everyone around him."

"So Peter was the one with the records?" Sadi asked. "Why was he so helpful?"

"And not the disc we took from The Orchid?" Alexa added.

"Your disc is important now, but only because Peter had a list of names. In fact, he has kept a detailed diary for over a year. Names, dates, shipments, everything."

"Do you think he planned to blackmail Gilner?" Jacob asked.

Rondell Gilner was the city councilman involved in the drug distribution ring. Alexa had recognized him, but Peter's diary gave them the evidence they needed to arrest him.

Blackwood looked at them all. "No, I think Peter just didn't trust anyone. If being a part of this group backfired on him, he had evidence he'd use to save himself."

"He was very much a loner, but one with big plans," Hank said. "He was packing to leave. He had a hundred thousand dollars hidden in his desk and his room."

Leave? Alexa bit her lip. So, with the kiss, Peter really was saying goodbye. And if she had waited to go after him, he might have gotten away.

"Wow!" Sadi, the lone tea drinker, poured herself another cup of the amber liquid from the little brown pot.

"He was smart, good-looking, ambitious, and Al says a very talented jazz piano player. We found a personal journal Peter kept, Al," Blackwood said. "His plan was to go to France for a few years, maybe play in nightclubs, then come back to New York City and start over."

"Do you think Lexie knew Peter was doing drugs?" Alexa asked.

"There's no way to know, Al," Blackwood said, "but it's ironic that his own sister's experimenting with Ecstasy, leading to her death, was what led us ultimately to Peter."

"The higher ups are impressed with your work, Alexa," Blackwood said.

"I don't feel that I really did that much," Alexa said.

"But you did. All your snooping made everyone, especially Gilner, nervous. If they had ignored you, we probably wouldn't have had enough proof to follow through. You forced their hand and they made too many mistakes. Not to mention that you were the one who recognized Peter. And he's providing enough evidence to put everyone behind bars for a long time."

"Yes, good work, Al," her father said again. "The people who do the funding have decided TIF really is a good idea. We might even get a little money for operating expenses, and you and Jacob and Hank, if he stays here with us, will get small, very small salaries. We plan to recruit more members. If you know anyone who is interested in police work, send them to us."

"Sadi?" Jacob smiled at her. "You with us?"

"My parents would never consent. You've heard of ghostwriters. I guess I'll be a 'ghost cop.' Someone has to look after Al."

Alexa smiled at Sadi. "I knew if I dialed you on my cell, and you couldn't reach me, you'd figure out that I'd gone to Peter's."

"Yep, I knew it and called Blackwood immediately when you didn't answer your phone. Wasn't that hard to second guess your next move would be to go talk to Peter." Sadi grinned. "I would have gone with you."

"I guess I needed to go alone. A part of my mind didn't believe that he was involved."

"You get to where it's hard to trust anyone." John Blackwood studied Alexa, his face serious. "You sure you want that burden?"

Alexa wasn't sure. All week her mind had spun with sadness, regret, the satisfaction of solving her first case, the up and down emotion of discovering someone she cared about not being who he seemed. Of actually being the criminal she was trying to smoke out. She almost smiled at her thoughts forming the word "smoke." She felt the smell was going to stay with her forever.

"I guess if I really need answers, I can consult a psychic." Alexa looked at Sadi and smiled.

Alexa had backed down on putting the tarot reading on her expense account, and then Madame Marie had also given back her money. But she might go get another reading. Marie had helped her think about her own strengths and, in a strange way, given her confidence.

"Emma was helpful in a small way with this case. We still don't know what's going to happen to her, to Amber and Bri." Alexa resolved to spend some quality time with Emma. She knew her sister was still grieving and finding out that Peter was involved with drug dealing in the high school had upset her, too.

"I figure the girls will get probation, or a deferred sentencing. They'll have time to sort through their actions and the consequences."

After everyone had gone home, Alexa found she was restless. Her father cleaned off the kitchen table and got out the backgammon set.

"You choose some music, Al. I don't feel like talking."

Her father knew she probably didn't want to talk, but she also didn't want to be alone in her room. Sometimes it was great to have a mind-reading father.

She looked over the CDs. Her hand didn't hesitate. She slipped *Kind of Blue* with Miles Davis on trumpet and Bill Evans on piano into the CD player. She suspected that even though she planned to continue with TIF, she was going to be kind of blue for a long time.